"Some things are just fated to be."

Lucas gave Chelsea an impatient glare. "We'll talk about this tonight," he said dismissively. "In the meantime, try not to shock my housekeeper more than she already is."

"I doubt that I could," Chelsea said, looking at Lucas beneath lowered lashes. "So far she's seen me returning your pajama jacket, leaving your bedroom in a sexy nightgown, and now she's seen us kissing each other. So unless she walks in on us making love, I don't think things could get any worse."

"I'm going back to work," he said, sounding exasperated. "I wish you would behave yourself."

"Do you?" she mocked, her head back in challenge.

Lucas gave her a look that spoke volumes before closing the door forcefully behind him as he left.

Poor Lucas. He obviously wasn't going to accept her love gracefully....

Books by Carole Mortimer

HARLEQUIN PRESENTS

These books may be available at your local bookseller.

Don't miss any of our special offers. Write to us at the following address for information on our newest releases.

Harlequin Reader Service
P.O. Box 52040, Phoenix, AZ 85072-2040
Canadian address: P.O. Box 2800, Postal Station A,
5170 Yonge St., Willowdale, Ont. M2N 6J3

CAROLE MORTIMER

cherish tomorrow

Harlequin Books

TORONTO • NEW YORK • LONDON
AMSTERDAM • PARIS • SYDNEY • HAMBURG
STOCKHOLM • ATHENS • TOKYO • MILAN

For
John, Matthew, and Joshua,
the three men in my life.

———————————————————

Harlequin Presents first edition July 1985
ISBN 0-373-10804-4

Original hardcover edition published in 1985
by Mills & Boon Limited

CHAPTER ONE

CHELSEA kept her head down against the driving rain, the suitcase she carried heavy in her hand, the cab driver having dropped her off a few buildings short of the one she wanted, despite the fact that she had shown him the slip of paper she had with Lucas's address written on it. And the fare had been exorbitant too, considering she had had to drag her own case in and out of the cab.

Not that she would have minded these few minutes respite from the rush and bustle of the last couple of days, if only it hadn't been raining. This trip to London had been unplanned, a last-minute thought of Jace's, and now that she was actually here and able to think a little more clearly herself she didn't think it was such a good idea. She hadn't seen Lucas McAdams for the last seven years, not since she was twelve years old, and she had no idea what he was going to make of her visit now. Jace had assured her it would be all right, and in Los Angeles it had seemed that it would be. Now that she was actually in London she wasn't so sure; Lucas may not even remember the small, silver-haired child whose huge blue eyes had once followed his every move. It had been an embarrassing time in Chelsea's life, one she would rather forget, although at least she could be confident Lucas had been unaware of her hero-worship; the only thing Lucas had been interested in seven years ago had been advancing himself up the legal ladder as quickly and as far as possible. And at twenty-seven his romantic interest had leant towards the sophisticated, usually patting Chelsea affectionately on the head before going out with one of those women when she visited his family with her parents.

A lot had happened in the intervening years, the move to California for Chelsea with her parents, their divorce six months ago, staying with her mother while continuing to see her father on a regular basis, the death of Lucas's own parents, while his young sister Camilla also moved to America to advance her modelling career. Camilla had remained a close friend to them all, had also encouraged this visit to Lucas, both she and Jace anxious to get Chelsea away from Los Angeles before the publicity broke out, sure that she would be well out of it with Lucas in London.

Well she was here now, and if Jace had sent the cable as he had said he would, then Lucas would be expecting her. She could always go on to a hotel later if it wasn't convenient with him for her to stay.

In her preoccupation with her troubled thoughts, her head bowed against the wind and rain, she didn't see the man getting out of the cab as she stepped sideways to avoid a puddle of water on the sidewalk, the suede boots she wore not the type she should get wet, the movement bringing her straight into the man's path, the force with which they collided coming as a complete shock to her, knocking all the breath from her body as she lost her balance, falling down on her bottom with a sickening jolt!

'Why didn't you look where you're going?' growled an unpleasantly harsh voice.

Chelsea gasped as she was verbally attacked

instead of given the concern she had been expecting. This man was as much to blame for the collision as she was! 'Help me up, would you, please?' she requested coldly, holding out her hand, aware that the seat of her denims was very wet, and her dignity was far from intact, as the people passing by stared at them curiously.

A lean hand came out to meet hers, and she was pulled effortlessly to her feet. 'Thank you,' she muttered as she brushed herself down with little effect, her denims damply creased, the thick sheepskin jacket she wore to keep out the brisk English November winds also damp. Her hair was secured under a thick woollen hat the same navy blue as her eyes, although the hat, too, was a little soggy from her walk in the rain.

She looked up at the man with a rueful shrug, at once struck by the handsome hauteur of his face, so tall that he dwarfed even her five-foot six frame. He was leanly built, seeming to be wearing a dark suit beneath the tailored overcoat. But it was his face her gaze returned to as if magnetised, dark brown hair styled over well-shaped ears, dark brown eyes looking down at her with a scowl, showing he wasn't nearly so impressed with her own appearance. His nose was long and straight, his mouth a stern line, harsh lines beside his nose and mouth, as if he had little to smile about in his life.

Chelsea couldn't help thinking that such a handsome man had no right to be so rude! 'I'm sorry,' she said automatically, although she knew the collision hadn't just been her fault.

The man nodded tersely, offering no words of apology himself as he turned abruptly to the right and entered the building there, a black overnight bag in his hand.

Chelsea picked up her own case with a frustrated glare in his direction, walking on several feet more before realising she, too, should have entered that apartment building. She only hoped that the rude man didn't turn out to be a friend of Lucas's; it would be a bad beginning.

The man was standing waiting for the descent of the elevator when she struggled through the entrance door with her case, sparing her only a cursory glance as not a hint of recognition entered the dark brown eyes. He had literally knocked her flying seconds before, and he had already dismissed her from his mind!

They stepped into the lift together, the only two occupants, the man pressing the button for the eighth floor before turning to her with polite query, his hand still poised next to the floor buttons.

'Eight suits me fine,' she murmured in a husky voice.

His haughtiness seemed to increase as he looked down his nose at her. 'Floor eight happens to be the penthouse apartments,' he told her in a harshly cold voice.

'Oh,' she nodded interestedly.

'It's private,' he added pointedly.

'Really?' she was determined to be polite, although this man's condescending manner was certainly pushing her to the limits of that politeness. What did it matter to him that she was going up to the eighth floor; he certainly didn't look as if he worked for the security! Maybe he was just one of those interfering neighbours who liked to know who everyone was and what they were doing here. Well, Lucas could be the one to tell him about her, if he chose to do so.

'Yes,' the word was bit out precisely, the man's manner more icy than ever.

'Nice,' she said appreciatively for the want of something better to say, wondering what this man expected of her. It was certainly an exclusive-looking building, she could tell that at a glance, but despite her casual appearance she was accustomed to a certain amount of luxury at home herself; no one could look their best after a ten-hour flight. Although looking at this man perhaps he would, he gave the impression—and she was sure it was a true one—that he always looked immaculate whatever the occasion, even the rain that had so dampened her hat had only slightly darkened his already dark hair.

The elevator had stopped on the eighth floor by this time, and with one finger pressed firmly on the 'Door Open' button the man made no move to get out. 'I believe you have the wrong floor,' he told her abruptly.

'I'm sure I don't,' she said equally as certainly, not needing to consult the piece of paper in her pocket to know this was where Lucas lived; she had looked at it enough during the flight.

The man's mouth twisted disdainfully. 'Let me put it another way——'

'I wish you would,' she sighed with weary impatience. 'I'm in a hurry.'

His mouth firmed now, his eyes coldly assessing. 'I'm not interested,' he stated icily.

'Sorry?' she frowned her puzzlement.

He sighed. 'This ploy may have worked with other men but I am not in the market for helping you find your air fare home. That was to be the routine, wasn't it?' he scorned.

'What routine?' Chelsea demanded impatiently. 'I don't know what you're talking about, I don't need an air fare. I only just got here.'

'And you are just about to leave again,' he told her with grim determination.

'I don't think so.' She shook her head.

'I do,' he nodded. 'You see, I was on to you the moment you entered the building.'

'On to me?' she repeated, her brain a little slow after her flight. 'Maybe you would care to explain that remark?'

'Certainly,' he bit out tautly. 'It was a wet night—a very wet night,' he added derisively. 'And you obviously need somewhere to stay tonight,' he looked pointedly at her suitcase. 'And I was unfortunate enough to be the one to bump into you.'

'At least you admit that now!'

'I admit nothing,' he ground out. 'We simply walked into each other, what I said just now was a matter of speech. But the moment you walked on after our collision, stopped, thought for a minute, and then turned back and came into the building after me was when I realised what you were doing.'

And she had thought he had entered the building without giving her a second glance, now it appeared he had been aware of her every movement. 'What was I doing?' she prompted, still puzzled by this conversation.

'Deciding I was a suitable candidate for you to spend the night with——'

'*What?*' she gasped disbelievingly, staring up at him as if he had gone insane, the rest of the conversation now falling into place. 'Now you listen here——'

'No, you listen,' he told her in a controlled voice, the brown eyes cold. 'You're too damned young to be up to tricks like this one——'

'"Tricks" being the operative word,' she

scorned angrily. 'That's what you thought you were going to be, didn't you, my "trick" for the night?'

His expression softened a little at her vehemence, although not much. 'I'm sure that you wouldn't have thought of it in that way——'

'Don't you believe it, buster,' Chelsea snapped, her eyes flashing darkly. 'What you're talking about is soliciting, and they're called hookers where I come from too!'

His expression became chilling. 'If you want to be basic——'

'Oh, let's be basic,' she derided furiously. 'You can tell me what my next move should be!' she challenged.

He shrugged broad shoulders, not at all disconcerted by her angry aggression. 'You watch which apartment I go into, leave it an appropriate amount of time, then knock on my door pretending you have the wrong address for the friend you were supposed to spend the night with, and that you would like to use the telephone. The telephone number conveniently turns out to be a false one too, and I'm supposed to offer to let you spend the night with me.'

'For a price!'

'Not necessarily, I've heard that picking pockets after the event is quite popular nowadays,' he commented calmly, looking at her with cool disdain.

'I don't know what sort of company you've been keeping,' she scorned. 'But I don't go through any man's pockets before *or* after the event. But you're right about one thing...'

'Yes?' he prompted arrogantly.

'I am here to visit a friend,' she nodded. 'And I doubt he would be at all amused by the wrong assumption you've just made about me!'

'You're saying you weren't looking for a bed for the night?' he derided mockingly.

'I'm saying I already have one!'

The brown eyes narrowed at her vehemence. 'This friend, what's his name?'

'I——'

'I think I should warn you, I know all the tenants on this floor,' he cut in softly.

'You would,' she shot him a resentful glance. 'But when I tell Lucas what you——'

'Lucas?' he echoed sharply, suddenly tense. 'You mean Lucas McAdams?'

'Yes,' she confirmed happily, glad to see how disconcerted he was by this disclosure.

'Where did you get that name from?' he demanded to know, his fingers biting into her arm as he tightly clasped it. 'Tell me!'

Chelsea tried to shake off his grasp, and failed. 'It happens to be the name of the friend I'm visiting. Now would you let go of my arm!' She tried to pry his fingers loose.

They wouldn't be moved, seeming to tighten if anything.

'Who told you he lived here?' he demanded briskly. 'There are no names listed downstairs, and the caretaker is too discreet to reveal the names of any of the tenants.'

'I told you——'

'That Lucas McAdams is a friend of yours,' his mouth twisted. 'I don't believe you.'

'And I don't give a damn what you believe!' Her eyes glittered with unshed tears, the last two days the worst of her life, this horrific scene with a complete stranger forcing her to breaking point. 'I *am* here to see him, and he *is* expecting me. If you would just——'

'I believe *I* would know if I were expecting a

young American guest,' he cut in with calm deliberation.

Chelsea's eyes widened with disbelief as the full implication of his words hit her. This man, this harshly suspicious man, couldn't possibly be Lucas McAdams! She remembered him as being youthfully handsome, rather serious, but not a man with a harsh hardness that repulsed as much as it attracted. But seven years ago she had been only twelve, still a child, with a crush on an older man, a man who had seemed almost god-like to her. At nineteen she could see that the ambition that had always been such a driving force in his life in the past, that had taken him to the top of his profession, had also taken all the youth and happiness from him and left only the harsh shell of a man. No wonder she hadn't recognised him; there seemed to be little of the old, exuberant Lucas left, just an automaton without a heart or soul.

'I thought that piece of information might surprise you,' he derided disdainfully.

'It did,' she nodded dully. 'You're nothing at all like I remember you.'

Impatience flared in the dark brown eyes. 'I think it's time to stop this game——'

'So do I,' she sighed wearily. 'You couldn't have got my father's message.'

'Don't you think——' he broke off, the arrogance replaced with confusion, then uncertainty, the hand that had been tightly gripping her arm moving slowly up to remove the woollen hat from her head. The long silver-blonde hair cascaded from its confinement to fall almost to her waist in gentle waves from the centre parting, giving her face an elfin appearance, her wide eyes framed by dark lashes, her nose short and pert, her mouth wide and full-lipped, her chin pointed. 'Chelsea ...?' Lucas spoke slowly, almost disbelievingly. 'Chelsea Stevens?'

'Yes,' she confirmed huskily, wishing they would get out of this elevator so that she could sit down, before she fell down.

Lucas seemed to become aware of their surroundings at the same time, making an impatient noise in his throat before guiding her over to one of the four doors leading off the long hallway, unlocking it quickly, glancing at the mail that lay on the table just inside the spaciously furnished apartment.

'You didn't get Jace's cable,' she repeated as she, too, saw the amount of letters lying there; there must be at least several days of mail.

'Obviously not,' he bit out dismissively, putting down his overnight case in the hallway. 'But now that you're here you can tell me what was in it.' His eyes narrowed as he looked across the room at her. 'Are you in trouble?'

'Pregnant, you mean?' She was passed being shocked by his suspicions about her.

'Yes,' he nodded.

'You know, at any other time I would find all this amusing,' she gave a wan smile, putting a hand up to her temple. 'But at this precise moment in time I don't think I could find anything funny.'

'Tell me,' he instructed abruptly.

'Do you mind if I take my coat off first?' The heat in the apartment was making her feel dizzy.

'Go ahead,' he invited, his eyes narrowed.

Chelsea shrugged out of the sheepskin jacket, feeling warm for the first time in days, too warm considering she was only wearing a thin black sweater under the jacket, Lucas taking the jacket from her as she looked around for somewhere to put it. 'Thanks,' she murmured gratefully, sitting down in one of the black leather armchairs without being invited to do so, her legs feeling too weak to support her any longer.

'Chelsea?' Lucas prompted impatiently, throwing the jacket down on another chair with his own, the three-piece suit he wore a charcoal grey colour, tailored to his magnificent physique, the waistcoat taut against his flat stomach, his shirt snowy white against his darker skin.

She took all this in about him without really being aware that she was doing so, her mind as numb as her emotions. How could she tell this man, this complete stranger, her reason for being here?

Lucas seemed to guess at her dilemma. 'Is it Jace?' His voice had gentled a little.

She shook her head. Jace was always the same, a handsome rogue of a man who succeeded in charming millions of viewers to his chat-show every week, one of the highest paid and well-liked men in television. No, Jace was indestructible.

'Gloria, then?' Lucas prompted again.

Her mother, an older more sophisticated version of herself, the silver-blonde hair kept in a shorter feathered style, faint lines about her blue eyes and vividly painted mouth disputing the mistake people often made of them being sisters. Gloria wasn't as strong and forceful as Jace, possessed a fragility of character and body.

'She's dead,' Chelsea stated flatly.

Lucas looked taken aback, almost disbelieving, as if he suspected her of lying.

And why shouldn't he, women of thirty-nine didn't just die, especially ones as beautiful as her mother had been. 'It's true,' she told him without emotion, her pale face pinched with sorrow now, dark shadows of pain in her eyes.

'Is that why Jace sent you here?' Lucas probed.

'Yes. He—I—The publicity. He didn't want me involved in that.' She moistened lips that suddenly seemed devoid of all feeling, having trouble articulating. 'He said he would contact you,' she repeated faintly.

'Maybe he did,' Lucas nodded grimly. 'I've been unreachable the last few days.'

She had guessed that from the overnight bag and the amount of mail waiting for him. 'Did you go anywhere nice?' she asked numbly.

'Chelsea——'

'Sorry,' she grimaced, the heat of the room suddenly overwhelming her. 'I'm so sorry,' she murmured vaguely just before she fainted.

She had no idea how much time had passed before she awoke to the feel of a hand gently tapping against her cheek, fighting back the blackness to find Lucas bending over her as she now lay full-length on the leather sofa, Lucas obviously having carried her here. He sat back as her eyes flickered open completely, a mask of polite concern making everything but his eyes seem emotionless, a depth of feeling in the brown eyes that he couldn't control or hide.

'I really am sorry.' She pushed her hair back from her face as she pushed herself up into a sitting position. 'I've never fainted before.'

'Your——' He broke off, his mouth firming in self-condemnation.

'My mother never died before,' Chelsea finished dryly. 'No, as far as I know I only had the one.'

'Chelsea!'

His anger had little effect on her, too much having happened to her the last few days for anything to have much effect, aware only that her mother was dead.

'I've made some coffee.' Lucas stood up to pour two cupfuls from the pot that stood on the silver tray on the low table in front of the sofa.

'Was I out that long?' Chelsea frowned.

'Long enough,' he nodded abruptly. 'Cream and sugar?'

'Milk if you have it, no sugar,' she told him in a preoccupied voice, barely aware of his leaving the room to come back with the jug of milk, although her shocked senses did register that the strong brew had sugar in despite her request. She grimaced. 'I said——'

'I heard you,' he confirmed shortly, lowering his long length into the chair opposite her. 'I think you need the glucose. When did you last have anything to eat?' His eyes were narrowed disapprovingly.

She knew she was pale, she had been since Saturday. 'Certainly not today,' she frowned in concentration. 'And not yesterday either.' She shook her head. 'I can't remember when I last ate,' she gave up even thinking about it, her head beginning to pound with the effort.

'Jace should have made sure that you did,' came the censorious reply.

Her mouth tightened. 'I think he may have had other things on his mind.'

Lucas didn't even blink an eyelid at the rebuke, his gaze steady. 'When did your mother die?'

She gulped down some of the coffee, not even noticing as it burnt her throat. 'Two days ago— no, it would be three now,' she belatedly remembered the time difference. 'We buried her this—*yesterday*, morning.'

'Had she been ill?' he probed. 'Your father didn't let me know——'

'How could he, if you've been unavailable?' she pointed out logically, guessing from the way he had avoided meeting her gaze earlier when he told her he had been away, that he had been with a woman. 'Jace couldn't have let you know, anyway,' she added dully. 'It was very sudden. The doctor diagnosed heart-failure.'

'At only thirty-nine?'

'It can happen at any age,' she shrugged. 'And she was never strong. Jace said there was nothing they could do.'

'I've never got used to the way you call your father Jace,' he shook his head.

'Why not, it's his name.' She had never seen anything strange about calling the handsome giant of a man who was her father by his first name; she had been doing it ever since she could remember. A young American on holiday in London he had met and married her mother in a matter of months, and she had entered the happy world of their marriage after only eighteen months together, both she and her mother moving back to America with Jace permanently when she was twelve years old. It seemed to have been the beginning of the decay of a previously happy marriage. 'What did you call your father?' she asked Lucas now to shake off the memory of past unhappiness.

'Sir, mostly,' he answered derisively, something like humour in the dark brown eyes, although it quickly faded. 'Look, I'd like to check on my post,' he frowned. 'Help yourself to more coffee; I shouldn't be long.'

Chelsea made no effort to stop him striding

from the room, needing the next few minutes alone to gather her shaken senses together. She had thought he would have received Jace's cable, hadn't envisaged having to tell him of her mother's death herself. She had withstood the shock of finding her mother unconscious in her bedroom, hours spent at the hospital with Jace before a doctor finally came out to tell them her mother was dead, the friends and well-wishers calling at the house to pay their respects, the funeral, and then finally Jace bundling her on the first available plane to England, little dreaming that the man he had sent her to wouldn't be here to receive her. The last few minutes of explaining things to Lucas had shaken her badly.

She hadn't even wanted to come here, had been too numb to protest her feelings when Jace had insisted she made herself scarce for when the news of her mother's death hit the media. But she wasn't numb now, and the thought of Lucas McAdams having her here on sufference, because of a friendship that, as far as she knew, hadn't been nurtured for the last seven years, filled her with dismay.

'Where do you think you're going?'

She turned guiltily, in the act of picking up her suitcase in preparation to leave, finding Lucas watching her from the doorway of the room he had disappeared into minutes earlier. 'I thought I'd go back to the airport,' she told him truthfully. 'And get the next flight home.'

His expression was darkly forbidding as he came back into the lounge. 'When you know Jace wants you to stay here?'

Her eyes widened. 'He did contact you?'

'Yes,' Lucas nodded, adding nothing to the confirmation.

'What did he say?' she prompted impatiently.

'Only what you've already told me,' he dismissed. 'He's going to telephone me once you've arrived. But he's already told me enough for me to realise this will be the best place for you for the next few weeks, at least,' he added grimly.

'I could have handled the publicity if Jace had given me the chance!'

'He wanted to spare you any unnecessary pain.'

'I'm sure he didn't tell you all that in a cable,' she derided defensively.

'You're right, he didn't,' Lucas bit out curtly. 'I know him well enough to be certain he would want to protect you at all costs.'

Chelsea was sure he was right, but she didn't know how he could make such a claim about a man he hadn't seen for so many years. 'Jace may have changed since you last saw him——'

'He hasn't.'

'Seven years is a long time.'

'I last met Jace in Los Angeles two weeks ago,' Lucas told her flatly.

Her brows rose as she couldn't hide her surprise. 'I didn't know that . . .'

Lucas shrugged. 'You live with your mother, so how could you possibly be aware of all your father's friends?'

Mainly because Jace had told her about most of them, although the remark Lucas had made about her living with her mother was what cast the shadow over her face. She had *lived* with her mother, she had no idea where she lived now, although it seemed that for the moment it was here, with this darkly handsome man who was a complete stranger to her!

'You're right,' she acknowledged dully. 'But

that friendship doesn't extend to me, and I would rather go back home.'

'You're wrong, Chelsea.' He shook his head, a hint of gentleness to the forbidding mouth. 'Even if I didn't at first remember you as the silver-haired angel who dogged my footsteps seven years ago I do remember you now, and I insist that you stay here.'

And she doubted many people resisted when this man insisted, and she was too weary to do so herself right now. 'You thought I was a hooker,' she reminded softly.

A dull red hue darkened his face beneath the prominent cheekbones. 'I'm sorry about that——'

'I'm not,' She shook her head, smiling wanly at his puzzled frown. 'Once I'm a little less tired, a little less numb, I'd like to think there's something we can sit down and laugh about together.'

Lucas looked as if he would rather forget about the whole incident than laugh about it, concentrating on the first thing she had said. 'The spare room is already made up, if you would like to go and lie down for a while?'

'You're sure I'm not going to inconvenience you?' she still hesitated.

'I'm sure,' he nodded.

'I meant with—a special friend, or someone,' she lamely tried to explain what she had meant; Lucas didn't come across as the sort of man that had *girlfriends*, although she was sure he had spent the past weekend with the current woman in his life. She vaguely wondered how serious the relationship was.

His mouth tightened disapprovingly. 'With no one,' he bit out. 'I'll show you your bedroom.'

Chelsea followed him with a slight grimace on her face; obviously she had touched on a delicate subject as far as this man was concerned. Maybe he just didn't like having to admit to the more basic urges and feelings that plagued the lives of other mortals!

Making rash judgments about her host wasn't going to make her stay here any easier! For all she knew Lucas could be very warm and loving to the woman he favoured with his attentions—She was doing it again! And she was too tired at the moment to make rational judgments about anything, especially this man; Jace had sent her here, so he must trust and like the other man. So would she.

'Camilla chose the decor in this room herself,' Lucas told her as he showed her into what was obviously his guest room, the pale lemon and brown colour scheme restful as well as being comfortably feminine; there was nothing Chelsea disliked more than a lot of frills and lace in a bedroom, having been pretty much a tomboy until she left school last year, still preferring to wear denims and tops when she wasn't at work. 'As my only female guest to date,' Lucas added pointedly.

She doubted that any female guest he had, other than family, would sleep in a separate bedroom to him anyway; he was much too old and experienced to settle for a platonic relationship. 'Camilla always did have good taste.' She ignored his last remark, although her normally effervescent nature wouldn't usually have let it go unchallenged. 'It's a lovely room.'

He nodded abruptly, putting her suitcase down on top of one of the single beds, uncaring of its dampness on the lemon coverlet. 'I hope you'll be comfortable. You have your own bathroom through here.' He opened a connecting door, the decor in there similar to the bedroom. 'Dinner will be in half an hour, if you would like something on a tray...?' he raised dark brows.

She shook her head. 'I'm not hungry. But I can cook you something, if you like?'

'That won't be necessary,' he dismissed arrogantly.

'I'd enjoy doing it.'

'I can get my own meals when necessary, although I have a housekeeper who usually leaves my evening meal for me. She'll be back at work from seven-thirty in the morning, and she doesn't leave until four. She's had the weekend off in my own absence,' he explained.

She should have known he didn't keep this huge apartment spotlessly clean himself; he hardly came over as the domesticated type. 'I can help her out, if that's okay?'

'Mrs Harvey would probably leave if you tried. And as she's been with me the last five years I wouldn't thank you for that,' he warned.

She could well imagine. 'I just thought that as well as being helpful it would give me something to do.' She shrugged. 'But if you say no...'

'I say no,' his mouth twisted. 'Good domestic help is hard to come by nowadays.'

He wasn't being patronising, merely stating a fact. Nevertheless, Chelsea wondered if the awesome-sounding Mrs Harvey viewed herself as 'domestic help'. She knew that their own maid, Clare, would have been most insulted by the title. Her face shadowed. Poor Clare, she had been as devastated by Gloria's death as everyone else; the elderly woman would probably never recover from the shock.

Lucas frowned as he watched the expressions flickering across her candid face. 'I'm not so sure you don't need food more than rest.'

And from the sound of it he personally intended seeing that she got it! But even the thought of food still made her feel ill, although she wasn't sure she had the strength to fight this formidable man right now. She was saved the trouble of finding the energy to try as the telephone began ringing somewhere in the apartment.

'I'll go and answer that,' he said somewhat impatiently.

'I'll probably have fallen asleep by the time you've finished with the call,' she told him hastily, in no mood to have food forced on her.

'Chelsea, I——' He broke off irritably as the telephone continued to ring shrilly, seeming to become more and more insistent the more he tried to ignore it. 'I'll have to go,' he strode to the door. 'If you need anything——'

'I'll find you,' she nodded.

Lucas gave her a hesitant look before leaving the room to answer the telephone, the melodious sound of his voice muffled through the apartment walls.

Chelsea sat down heavily on the single bed next to her now that she was alone, the weight of her mother's death forcing her down, both mentally and physically. She would never, ever, forget finding her beautiful mother lying so peacefully in her bed she seemed to be only sleeping, her silver-gold hair spread out across her pillow as if brushed there, the blue of the silky nightgown she wore a perfect match for the eyes beneath the long, fanned-out lashes, her make-up perfect, her mouth seeming to be curved into a smile, almost a secretive smile, as if something pleased her even as she lay there.

But that serene beauty had been disturbed from the moment Chelsea had contacted the emergency services. Her mother had no longer looked peaceful or beautiful as they tried to revive life where it had decided it no longer wished to be.

And it had all been her fault. If she hadn't decided to go bowling straight from work instead of going home as she had planned to do her mother might still be alive now, she might have been able to get the help soon enough to be of some good to her mother. It hadn't seemed so strange when she received no reply at home when she called to tell her mother of her delay; since the two of them had lived alone they had lived pretty independent lives, both of them busy with new careers. She had simply assumed her mother had gone out to an early supper, her job as a realtor often keeping her late with prospective clients. She hadn't dreamt, hadn't guessed, the real reason her mother had been unable to come to the telephone. To come home and find her like that had shaken Chelsea to the core. She doubted she would ever get over not being there when her mother needed her the most. She knew with certainty that the guilt would always be with her.

CHAPTER TWO

THE shower she had taken had refreshed her a little, and although she still didn't feel like eating, the thought of another cup of coffee—her staple diet of the last few days—seemed like a good idea.

She could still hear Lucas on the telephone as she stepped out into the hallway, it hadn't seemed worth the bother of dressing again so soon after undressing. Besides, the black towelling robe she wore was adequate clothing for the brief time she needed to leave her room.

'—you know I've enjoyed the last few days,' Lucas was saying impatiently as she tried to pass through the lounge unnoticed. 'All right, a *very* enjoyable time,' he added huskily after a brief pause. 'But I've already explained to you, several times, that I can't possibly go out and leave Chelsea alone tonight.'

She had come to an abrupt halt at the sound of her name, blatantly listening to the rest of the conversation. If Lucas thought he had to baby-sit her he was mistaken!

'God, Jennifer, you're a mature woman of thirty-two, what attraction do you think a nineteen-year-old girl would hold for me?' he answered the woman on the telephone exasperatedly.

Chelsea knew half-a-dozen men of his age, a couple of work colleagues, and some friends of her father, who definitely didn't think of her as a *girl*!

Lucas seemed to become aware of her

indignation emanating across the room at that moment, turning from his sightless gazing out of the window, his mouth tightening disapprovingly as he took in her appearance, her damp hair, the black robe, her bare legs and feet. 'I'll call you back, Jennifer,' he spoke woodenly into the mouthpiece, his gaze still locked icily on Chelsea. 'No, I'm not being difficult,' he sighed as the woman obviously objected. 'I'll just have to call you back.' He put down the receiver without waiting for a reply.

Chelsea braced her shoulders as if ready for battle as she and Lucas faced each other across the room. 'I was just on my way to the kitchen to get some coffee,' she told him defensively.

Lucas shrugged. 'Feel free to help yourself to anything you want while you're staying here,' he invited.

He was waiting for something else, and they both knew it. 'You don't have to alter your plans because of me,' she said huskily. 'If you intended going out tonight then please do so, I'm just going to fall into bed and go to sleep anyway.'

He shook his head. 'My plans to see Jennifer were not definite ones.'

'But you've just spent the last few days with her, haven't you?' Chelsea frowned at his casual dismissal of the other woman.

His mouth tightened. 'Chelsea——'

'Sorry.' She held her hands up in apology. 'Please forget I said that, it's really none of my business. But she does sound like a good friend, and I certainly don't need the company.'

The brown eyes narrowed in surprise. 'Are you dismissing me?'

She flushed. 'No, I—Yes, perhaps I am,' she conceded ruefully. 'Although I didn't mean to.

But when I asked if I would be making things awkward for you by staying here you said no,' she reminded softly.

'And you aren't. Jennifer has been a friend of mine for some time, but she has no claims on me, as I have none on her. I certainly don't have to justify my actions to her, or to anyone else,' he stated arrogantly.

She was sure he didn't either. Although the fact that the woman Jennifer had been a 'friend' for some time looked as if she didn't normally mind that. 'I'd really rather you kept your dinner date,' she told him huskily. 'I'm not going to be any company at all, feeling as tired as I do.'

He seemed to hesitate, finally shrugging agreement. 'Maybe you're right.'

'I know I am.' She nodded, relieved that she hadn't had to try too hard to persuade him to go out. The last thing she needed was this complete stranger hovering over her.

He nodded. 'I'll leave the telephone number on the pad where I can be reached if you should need me.'

'I'm not a child, Lucas,' she told him stiffly.

His cold gaze raked over her from head to foot. 'I can see that,' he grated. 'But you have had a severe shock, and——'

'And I'm not likely to run around the apartment shrieking hysterically,' she taunted. 'The doctor gave me some pills,' she sighed. 'Maybe I'll take a couple,'

Lucas frowned. 'What sort of pills?'

She shrugged. 'Just something to relax me.'

'Tranquilisers?' his frown deepened.

'I guess,' she nodded, wondering what all the fuss was about now.

'I don't like the idea of leaving you here under the influence of drugs.'

Angry colour flamed in her cheeks. 'So now I'm a drug addict?' she demanded in an exasperated voice. 'First I'm a hooker, and now I'm a drug-addict!'

Lucas's mouth tightened. 'I wasn't——'

'Two prescribed pills do not make me an addict!' Her voice rose shrilly as she finally began to crack under the strain. 'I just need something to relax me a little. God, my mother only died three days ago!'

'I know, Chelsea. I know.' He walked over to clasp her shoulders, looking down at her with sympathetic eyes. 'But I think a brandy might have the same effect.'

'Aren't you frightened I might become an alcoholic?' she asked tautly.

His face darkened. 'Chelsea——'

'I just want to go to sleep, can't you understand that?' Tears blinded her as she looked up at him. 'I *need* to sleep. That way I don't have to remember,' her voice broke.

Lucas's hands tightened painfully on her shoulders before he pulled her firmly into his arms, cradling her body against the firmness of his. 'I'm sorry.' He stroked her silvery hair. 'I think this has all been more of a shock to me than I realised.'

She bent her head back to look at him. 'You?' she frowned, blinking back the tears, unable to see this man as anything but completely controlled.

'I cared for your mother too,' he bit out tautly.

Her mouth twisted. 'Don't tell me you were seeing her secretly, too?'

Lucas released her abruptly, stepping back.

'None of my visits to Jace were made in secret. And I hadn't seen your mother for several years, to answer your question. Although that doesn't mean I can't feel saddened by her death.'

It was a verbal rebuke, and yet Chelsea couldn't apologise for what she had said. It wasn't like Jace not to tell her things, and he hadn't mentioned Lucas McAdams since they left England seven years ago.

She nodded abruptly. 'I'll just get my coffee and go back to my room.'

'Chelsea...'

Her face was expressionless as she looked at him. 'Yes?'

Whatever he had been about to say he changed his mind, his mouth firming into a thin line as his gaze raked over her mercilessly. 'If we're going to be living in close proximity for some time then I suggest we establish a few ground rules,' he told her tautly.

She stiffened expectantly. 'Yes?'

'In the first place I would suggest that we respect each other's privacy.'

Colour heightened her cheeks at the rebuke. 'And secondly?' she prompted abruptly.

'Secondly, I would appreciate your wearing a little more than you have on now outside the privacy of your bedroom,' he bit out harshly.

The colour deepened in her cheeks, making her look very young. 'I'm perfectly respectable,' she defended.

'I didn't say you weren't,' he dismissed. 'And you are far from the first woman I've seen partially, or indeed fully, unclothed. I just happen to think it would make things a little more—acceptable.'

'To whom?'

'To anyone who cares to be interested,' he came back irritably.

She was too tired to remind him that only minutes ago he had claimed that he didn't have to justify his actions to anyone; it was his apartment, he had the right to make any rules about their living together that he cared to. 'I can accept that,' she shrugged, sure this man was too 'proper' to leave his own bedroom without sufficient clothing, even when he was alone here. It seemed incredible that he was the man she had found so exciting in her pre-teen years; he now appeared too staid and respectable for such an interest, despite his good looks.

'Good,' he bit out. 'Then I suggest you get your coffee and go to bed.'

She hadn't been spoken to in this condescending manner since she was a child—if then! Her parents had always treated her like a person in her own right, even to the extent of fully examining her feelings on the subject before they decided to get a divorce. Lucas treated her as if she didn't have a brain of her own.

Nevertheless, she made no demur, too tired and worn at this moment to argue her maturity. When the shock of her mother's death receded a little it would be a different matter!

Lucas had gone from the lounge when she returned from the kitchen, and she could only assume he had gone to his own room to prepare for his date with Jennifer. She couldn't help wondering about the other woman. A mature woman of thirty-two, Lucas had called her on the telephone. Was that all he wanted in his arms, maturity? Chelsea didn't doubt Jennifer would be beautiful, and that she would also be sophisticated enough to conduct an affair with Lucas, because the relationship was obviously a physical one. But would she be nice, warm, or would she possess that remoteness that made Lucas so alien to those about him, made him seem removed? Probably the two of them would never meet, although Jennifer sounded as if she would like to see her.

'I forgot to give you the brandy——' Lucas broke off awkwardly as he entered her bedroom without knocking, his mouth tightening disapprovingly as her unbelted robe showed she wore nothing beneath it. 'I'm sorry,' he said abruptly. 'I had no idea ... I thought you would be in bed,' he rasped, his jaw rigid.

'I just cleaned my teeth.' She handled the situation so much more calmly than he, retying the belt on her robe with hands that shook only slightly. And that wasn't just because for a moment, a very brief moment, she had seen acknowledgment of her as a woman in the dark brown depths of his eyes; his own appearance was much more devastating. The black evening suit and snowy white shirt made him appear taller and broader than ever, and so handsome he took her breath away.

'I see,' he harshly acknowledged her statement. 'I forgot to give you the brandy.' He held up a glass with about an inch measure in it. 'This should help you sleep.'

Her eyes widened. 'That much should knock me out!' she derided. 'Believe it or not, I rarely, if ever, touch alcohol.'

His expression darkened. 'Chelsea——'

'Thank you for the brandy,' she hastily interrupted the reprimand she had invited by her mockery. 'I'll drink it in a moment.'

'You haven't taken the tablets yet?'

Her mouth tightened; did he think she was completely stupid! 'No.'

'Good,' he nodded curtly, holding out the glass to her with a long, lean hand.

Chelsea took it with unsteady fingers, feeling angered by this further display of arrogant authority, wishing Jace had never sent her here, although understanding the reason that he had. But that didn't make Lucas's behaviour any easier to bear. 'Thanks,' she told him abruptly. 'And I think perhaps we ought to establish another ground rule.' Her head was back defiantly, 'I won't walk into your bedroom without first knocking if you won't walk into mine.'

A dark hue coloured his lean cheeks. 'I wasn't thinking when I did that, it won't happen again.'

She instantly felt contrite for being rude when he had offered her his hospitality. 'I'm sorry,' she sighed. 'It seems Jace has put us both in an awkward position by imposing on you in this way.'

'When you're family it isn't an imposition,' he replied in a preoccupied voice.

'Family ...?' she frowned. 'I would hardly say your friendship with Jace makes me that.'

Lucas straightened, nothing preoccupied about him now. 'I've known you almost from the moment you were born, I feel like your uncle,' he dismissed abruptly.

'Feeling like one and actually being one are two different things,' she snapped, chagrined that he still continued to treat her like a child. He had a shock coming to him when she was feeling more like herself; she didn't always wear the casually youthful clothing she had arrived in, could be sophisticated herself when she needed to be, or wanted to be. And Lucas's attitude was making her want to be more and more.

Lucas's expression was guarded as he looked at her. 'Nevertheless, that's what I feel like,' he insisted coldly. 'Are you sure you're going to be all right while I'm out?' he abruptly closed the subject.

'I'll be fine,' she nodded.

'I won't be too late,' he told her as he walked to the door, the gold cufflinks gleaming brightly at his wrists as his hand came up to open it.

'Don't hurry back on my account,' she shrugged.

'I won't,' he snapped.

Chelsea sighed as he took offence at her words. 'Lucas ...'

'Yes?' his eyes were narrowed.

'I—I—Oh God!' Her control finally crumpled, her legs giving out weakly beneath her as she fell to the carpeted floor, her face buried in her hands as tears streamed down her cheeks.

She tried to resist the strong arms that pulled her to her feet, but Lucas was remorseless in his intent, holding her tightly against the hardness of his chest as deep shudders wracked her body as she continued to cry. She cried until she had no more tears left to cry, loud agonised sobs as the pain of losing her mother ripped through her. And as she cried Lucas just continued to hold her, not saying a single word, just supporting her in his strong arms.

'I'm sorry,' she gulped at last, raising her head to see with dismay the huge damp patch she had made on his jacket and shirt, the black bow-tie at his throat looking slightly limp too. 'Oh God, look what I've done,' she groaned, brushing down the damp material.

'Leave it,' Lucas instructed curtly.

'But I've messed up your——'

'I said leave it, Chelsea.' He grasped her arms, holding her in front of him. 'Do you think I care about being slightly damp?'

A wan smile twisted her mouth. 'A *lot* damp,' she corrected.

'It doesn't matter,' he dismissed. 'I have other suits.'

'That isn't the point——'

'I agree,' he bit out tightly. 'It isn't.' He held her gaze with steady intensity.

Her cheeks coloured with embarrassment as she avoided that gaze. To have emotionally broken down in the presence of a man she no longer knew seemed to her the height of embarrassment, to be verbally made aware of it, no matter how well intentioned, was unacceptable to her at this moment. 'I've kept you long enough,' she dismissed flatly.

Lucas looked at her searchingly for several long minutes before nodding abruptly. 'I'll leave you to rest. Mrs Harvey will be here at seven-thirty in the morning; she'll get your breakfast for you whenever you care to get up. Take your time, there's no rush.'

'I don't want to be any trouble.'

'You won't be,' he assured her arrogantly. 'Camilla stays with me for weeks at a time when she's working in London.'

'It isn't the same,' Chelsea mumbled, wishing he could see and understand that. Or maybe he did, and just ignored the fact. And she didn't have the strength to pursue it after her bout of crying, just wanting to fall into bed.

Lucas seemed to guess her plight, going to the door. 'If you need me during the night I'm just across the hall from here. Don't hesitate,' he added sternly. 'You won't be disturbing me,

I'm a very light sleeper,' he told her before he left.

And after already crying all over him once tonight she had no intention of disturbing his sleep, not for any reason. She had coped with her grief in her own way so far, and she didn't intend to change that.

Which made the fact that she had broken down in front of Lucas in the way she had all the more surprising. She hadn't cried once since the nightmare began, not when she found her mother, and not when they told her she was dead either. She couldn't think what had prompted her to collapse in front of Lucas of all people; he wasn't exactly an emotional man himself. Whatever the reason for her breakdown she didn't intend letting it happen again.

The harsh November rain was still falling against the window when she woke the next morning, completely disorientated until she remembered she was in Lucas's apartment, in his spare bedroom. And with that realisation came the renewed pain of her mother's death.

She had drunk the brandy Lucas gave her the night before, had miraculously fallen asleep almost immediately she got into bed. The clock on the bedside table told her it was nine-thirty; she had almost slept the clock round!

Lucas had no doubt already left for the plush office Camilla had told her he had somewhere in town, and the invaluable Mrs Harvey would be in the apartment. Chelsea fleetingly wondered what he had told his housekeeper about her, the truth would be preferable as far as she was concerned. Although what little she had learnt about Lucas the evening before she doubted he felt he had to explain his actions, or those of his guests, to a mere employee.

It wasn't until she threw back the bedclothes to go through to the bathroom that she gasped her dismay. She was wearing a black silk pyjama jacket that hadn't been there when she fell into bed the evening before! And it could only belong to one person, Lucas! It was much too big for her slender frame, hung precariously off one shoulder, the sleeves turned back to accommodate her shorter arms, the length of it reaching almost down to her knees. And it smelt vaguely of the elusive aftershave Lucas had worn the evening before.

She had been sleepwalking in the nude!

There could be no other explanation for her to wake up in Lucas's pyjama jacket. She had often walked in her sleep when she was a child, but much less so now that she was older, and it hadn't really mattered that she did when there was just her mother and herself at home.

That the trauma of the last few days had brought on one of the rare occasions when it happened she had no doubt. And she blushed with embarrassment at the thought of Lucas having to cover her nakedness with his own pyjama jacket before guiding her back to bed. Whatever must he think of her! More to the point, how was she supposed to face him again after this? He might, as he said, have seen plenty of other women unclothed, but the circumstances of him seeing her made her writhe with embarrassment.

And uninvited came the question, had he liked what he had unwittingly seen?

It was a provocative thought, and one that she regretted as soon as it came into her mind. It put their relationship on too personal a level, and it was going to be difficult enough to maintain the tenuous link they had now without any added complications, such as her possibly rekindling the attraction she had once felt for him.

Nevertheless, the colour in her cheeks refused to recede as she showered and dressed, and she could only hope that Lucas had indeed left for the day; she had no idea what sort of hours lawyers kept in England.

A glance out of her bedroom window showed her that the central heating in the apartment was deceiving, that it was still very cold and wet, so she put on fitted blue trousers and a designer blouse in a beautiful rust colour. The wealth and publicity of her father's career may have helped to destroy her parents' marriage, it had also given Chelsea a taste for beautiful clothing that had always been indulged. She had been limited as to the amount of clothing she could bring with her on this trip, had had little inclination for packing, but at home she had a wardrobe full of designer-label clothing. A spoilt brat, she thought with a grimace. Oh well, she was what she was.

Her long hair was still slightly damp from her shower, but she knew from experience that the silvery fine hair would soon dry; its long silver length made a startling contrast to the rust colour of her blouse. Her eyes were still shadowed by grief, but at least the sleep seemed to have given her back some of her usual confidence, the ability to cope, and she knew that during the weeks and months that were to follow she would need every ounce of that confidence.

She made her bed before leaving her room, the door to Lucas's bedroom firmly closed, the lounge empty, the only sounds to be heard coming from the kitchen. Bracing her thin shoulders in expectation Chelsea entered the room.

A middle-aged woman looked up from the vegetables she was peeling to put into the huge roasting pot on the table in front of her, the woman's expression becoming as wary as Chelsea's own.

'Good morning,' Chelsea greeted lightly.

'Miss Stevens,' the woman acknowledged abruptly.

'Chelsea, please,' she returned smoothly.

'Miss Chelsea,' the woman nodded abruptly, tall and thin, her short curled hair a very light brown colour, beginning to grey at her temples.

'No, I meant——'

'Can I get you some breakfast now?' Mrs Harvey turned to wipe her hands on the towel, a pristine white pinafore covering her severely styled blue dress. 'Mr McAdams had his meal some time ago.'

There was no rebuke in the words for her own tardiness, just a statement of fact. 'Lucas is here?' she asked half in anticipation, half in dread, the memory of that sensuous black silk against her flesh, and its reason for being there, still too new for her to be able to look forward to seeing him again.

The housekeeper shook her head. 'He always leaves at precisely eight-fifteen,' her voice was flat as she stated her employee's movements.

Chelsea mentally concluded that Lucas lived his life in altogether too precise a manner, that the last seven years had made him cold and unemotional. Or perhaps a woman had brought about the change. Maybe he had once been very badly hurt and now preferred to live his life in this stiffly rigid pattern that allowed no room for a woman *to* hurt him; Jennifer didn't sound as if she had penetrated his emotions, just his need for sexual fulfilment. Somehow Chelsea couldn't even imagine Lucas with ruffled hair and a flushed face of satiation after the throes of lovemaking. Probably even that was an auto-motive reflex to him!

'I'll just have a slice of toast and some coffee,' Chelsea answered Mrs Harvey as she realised she was still looking at her expectantly.

She nodded. 'If you would like to go through to the dining-room I'll bring it through to you.'

'Oh I didn't mean for you to get it——'

'It's what I'm here for,' the woman insisted, her light blue eyes wide with indignation.

Chelsea shook her head. 'You're here to take care of Lucas, not any unexpected guests that suddenly appear,' she smiled so that the woman shouldn't once more take offence.

'I'm perfectly capable of getting breakfast for two people instead of one,' Mrs Harvey snapped as she prepared the coffee perculator.

The housekeeper had taken offence despite all her efforts, and with a shrug of resignation Chelsea pulled out one of the chairs at the kitchen table and sat down. 'I'd rather sit in here and eat if you don't mind?' Once again she gave a friendly smile.

The woman looked surprised. 'I'm sure you would be more comfortable in the dining-room.'

Chelsea shook her head. 'This is just fine,' she insisted, envisaging nothing more dismal than sitting alone in that huge dining-room, where everything was tidily in its place, with not a speck of dust anywhere. At least here in the kitchen the apartment looked lived in, an orderly clutter on the work units as Mrs Harvey prepared the food for the evening meal.

The housekeeper shrugged. 'If that's what you want.' But she didn't look very comfortable with the idea of a guest sitting in her kitchen to eat toast and drink coffee.

Chelsea sipped the coffee greedily, the brandy Lucas had insisted she drink the evening before leaving her mouth feeling like sandpaper, even after cleaning her teeth twice. But Lucas had been right about its effect on her; she had slept soundly. At least, she had thought she had! The hot colour returned to her cheeks as she thought of the black pyjama jacket that lay across her bedroom chair.

'Lucas said you've worked for him for five years,' she burst into speech with the first thing that came into her mind, not wanting to dwell on the memory of last night.

'Yes.' The other woman had returned to her preparation of dinner after giving Chelsea her breakfast.

'That's a long time,' she added conversationally.

'Yes.'

'I imagine Lucas is nice to work for.' She tried once again to draw the other woman into conversation.

'He's a very thoughtful employer,' Mrs Harvey confirmed abruptly.

Because he didn't want to lose his 'domestic help'? She couldn't believe Lucas was as unfeeling about people as he liked to appear to be. 'I imagine so,' she answered in a preoccupied voice. 'Will he be home for lunch?'

The housekeeper frowned at the suggestion. 'He doesn't usually—But perhaps with you here?' she added uncertainly.

Chelsea shook her head, her hair moving silkily

against her slender back. 'I'm sure Lucas won't alter his routine for me.' She stood up to pour herself some more coffee, receiving a disapproving look for her action. 'Our maid at home doesn't usually mind my getting my own coffee,' she excused lamely.

'I imagine a lot of things are done differently in America.' Mrs Harvey stiffly passed her the jug of milk.

The middle-aged woman somehow made it sound as if she suspected all sorts of decadence occurred in the other country. 'I imagine they are,' Chelsea smiled, having felt the same nervousness herself about an alien country seven years ago when her parents had decided to make the move to her father's homeland. As it had turned out she loved it over there. 'So you don't think Lucas will be home for lunch?' she persisted.

'I can't say for certain,' Mrs Harvey frowned. 'He doesn't inform me of his every move.'

'I think I'll risk it and go out anyway,' Chelsea decided.

'Oh, I don't think he expected you to leave the flat today,' the housekeeper said worriedly. 'His last instruction was that I was to see that your day here was comfortable.' The woman looked concerned that she may already have disobeyed that instruction.

And Chelsea was well aware of the reason Lucas had made it; he didn't want her to possibly see a newspaper. She had been aware of the absence of all such literature both in the lounge and here, and yet she was sure Lucas was one of those men who read several newspapers as he ate his breakfast. The story of her mother's death would be front-page news in America once the information leaked out, and she didn't doubt it would be the same over here. Being protective was one thing, it was the reason she had let Jace send her here after all, but she didn't intend becoming a self-inflicted prisoner in Lucas's apartment; she would go insane in a matter of hours, needed to get out, to have breathing space.

'And it has been,' she assured the other woman warmly. 'I just need some air.'

'But——'

'Don't worry about me, Mrs Harvey,' she deliberately interrupted the other woman. 'It may have been some time, but I used to live here.'

Light blue eyes widened in surprise at this information. 'You did?'

'Yes,' Chelsea laughed softly. 'I was born here. Have I lost my accent so completely?'

Mrs Harvey's expression softened a little. 'Well, no, I suppose not, not now I think about it. But Mr McAdams said an American guest...'

'I suppose I am now,' she shrugged. 'But when I lived here seven years ago I knew London quite well.'

'We're slow-moving over here; you'll find it hasn't changed much!'

'That's what I'm hoping,' Chelsea smiled.

The frown returned to the older woman's brow. 'I'm sure Mr McAdams would rather you stayed here today, in fact I'm sure he assumed that you would.'

'Don't worry.' She stood up. 'I'll tell Lucas it was all my own idea.'

'That isn't the point——'

'The point is, Mrs Harvey,' cool determination entered her voice, 'that if I don't soon get out of here I shall go quietly insane!'

Compassion entered the light blue eyes.

'Maybe you should just rest today,' her voice had softened noticeably. 'You must be very tired.'

And suddenly Chelsea knew that the housekeeper was well aware of the reason for her visit. No doubt Lucas had asked the other woman to keep a friendly eye on her. And she just wished everyone would stop treating her like a child who couldn't accept the truth!

'I'm fully rested,' she stated stubbornly. 'And now I intend going out.' She turned and left the room, sure that the housekeeper would instantly telephone Lucas. But she would already have left by the time he was able to stop her.

The black silk pyjama jacket caught her gaze as she pulled on her thick sheepskin coat, frowning as she debated whether or not she should return it to Lucas's room or leave it here. She didn't doubt that despite having made the bed and tidied the bedroom that Mrs Harvey would come in later and clean in here. And Lucas's pyjama jacket in her room looked very suggestive, too suggestive to just leave there.

She picked up the sensuous-feeling garment and crossed the hall to Lucas's room, entering quietly, the decor in here as she had imagined it would be, stark and masculine in brown and white, not warm and inviting as the room Camilla had decorated was.

There was little in this room to actually say it was occupied, just a leather jewellery box on the dressing-table and a picture of Camilla next to it, several paperbacks on the bedside table; with no sign of the bottom part of the black pyjamas! The double bed with its brown quilt was already made, the adjoining bathroom that could be seen through the open door was meticulously clean and tidy. Her own untidyness was likely to drive Lucas to drink in a week!

A week? How long was she going to be here? No time had been set for her visit, but she didn't intend imposing on Lucas for too long.

She blushed guiltily as she turned to find Mrs Harvey watching her from the doorway. 'I—er—I came to return this,' she indicated the jacket she had left on the chair, her blush deepening as she realised how that must sound. 'Lucas lent it to me when I realised that in my haste I had forgotten to pack a nightgown,' she excused lamely, not wanting to have to admit the real reason she had been in possession of half Lucas's pyjama set, although she knew the explanation she was giving now was even more damning than the truth, giving the impression of an intimacy that just wasn't there.

Blue eyes were sceptical, although Mrs Harvey didn't dispute or question the explanation. 'I've just spoken to Mr McAdams, and he is coming home to lunch after all, so he would like you to be here.'

The hasty telephone call to Lucas had been expected, so she showed no surprise. 'What time will he be home?'

'About twelve-thirty——'

'Well it's only eleven o'clock now, so I have plenty of time for a walk.'

'But——'

'I'll see you later, Mrs Harvey,' she called out lightly as she quickly let herself out of the apartment, heaving a sigh of relief once she was out in the carpeted hallway.

The escalator was already coming up when she pressed the button, the young man already occupying it stepping to one side as she entered.

Chelsea acknowledged his appreciative gaze with a cool lift of her chin; she certainly wasn't in the mood for a flirtation. But the man continued to look at her, and she couldn't help but be aware of how attractive he was, overlong blond hair styled back from a centre parting, twinkling blue eyes watching her interestedly, his tall body athletic.

And then something occurred to her. 'Weren't you going up?' she frowned, knowing the eighth floor was the top one.

'Yes,' he admitted, following her out on to the ground level.

'But you came down again,' she pointed out needlessly.

'Yes.'

'Why?' she still frowned her puzzlement.

'Because you did,' he told her happily. 'I couldn't pass up the opportunity of getting to know Lucas's guest; he would never introduce you to me himself.'

'Lucas told you I was staying at his apartment?' It didn't sound like the Lucas she knew!

'Let's just say that there isn't much that can be kept secret in a building like this one,' he shrugged. 'I'm John Anderson, by the way.'

'Chelsea Stevens,' she replied in a preoccupied voice. 'Do you live here?'

'Why else would I be going up in the lift?' he gently teased.

'Why else?' she ruefully acknowledged the stupidity of her question.

'I know this may sound a bit forward from someone you just met,' he said slowly. 'But would you like to join me for a cup of coffee?'

She looked at him frowningly. Why not? After all, he did know Lucas, and there could be no harm in having coffee with him. She nodded wordlessly.

CHAPTER THREE

'So how long have you known Lucas?' She absently stirred milk into the coffee they had ordered in a cafe in the centre of the city, a large noisy cafe that suited Chelsea's mood perfectly.

They had taken a cab from the quietly exclusive residential area into the rush and bustle of the shopping areas, Chelsea having forgotten how noisy and crowded it could be after the relative peace and quiet of the beach-side house she shared with her mother. She felt relieved to have John to help her, having forgotten a lot of other things about London too, starting with the fact that she had very little English money with her, only what Camilla had kept from her last trip here, having left on too short a notice to be able to get any pounds from a bank.

John looked at her with steady blue eyes. 'I don't think I did say I know him,' he said quietly.

Her frown returned. 'But you spoke as if you did.'

'Maybe,' he shrugged. 'But I'm sure I didn't say that I did. Relax,' he soothed as she stiffened. 'Now do I look as if I have rape in mind?' he mocked. 'I would hardly take my "victim" out for coffee first!'

She smiled ruefully as she realised how ridiculous that thought was. 'Sorry,' she grimaced. 'The last couple of days haven't been all that easy for me; I'm tending to over-react at the moment.'

His gaze was steady. 'I would say that's understandable in the circumstances.'

Chelsea knew she paled, her eyes huge blue pools. 'What do you mean?' she asked cautiously.

'I'm afraid your picture is in most of the national dailies today,' he told her gently.

She swallowed hard, looking about her self-consciously. But no one seemed to be taking any undue notice of them, all getting on with their own lives, their own problems.

'Don't look so hunted.' John's hand came out to cover hers as it rested on the table. 'No one expects to see the daughter of Jace and Gloria Stevens sitting in a London cafe!'

Her troubled gaze returned to his. 'And yet you recognised me?'

He shrugged. 'I told you, not much is kept secret in a building like the one we just left.'

'Lucas isn't going to be pleased.' She remembered the way he had tried to prevent her leaving the apartment; obviously he had known the story had broken and he hadn't wanted her to run the risk of recognition. He was going to be *far* from pleased that she had gone out anyway!

'You can't stay hidden forever,' John pointed out logically.

'No,' she acknowledged.

'Just out of curiosity, why *are* you hiding?' John frowned, his handsome face puzzled.

'Because of my father's misplaced sense of protection,' she grimaced.

'What does he think you need protecting from?'

Chelsea sighed. 'The media, I would imagine. You've seen the newspapers,' she shrugged. 'My mother's death was a tremendous shock to us all.'

'None of you knew about her condition?'

'No,' her answer was sharp. 'If we had we could perhaps have stopped it happening.'

'How?'

'Well I don't know that!' her voice rose sharply. 'I just think maybe we could.'

'I'm sorry,' John said gently. 'I'm being insensitive.'

Not really. He was simply asking the questions a lot of other people would like answers to. And she didn't really have any. No wonder Jace had wanted her out of the way! She probably would have let him down.

'No, you aren't,' she sighed. 'But I don't think any of us realised there was anything wrong with my mother, certainly not enough to cause her death.'

'Perhaps it was the divorce that was such a strain on her,' John shrugged.

Chelsea's eyes widened. 'You seem to know an awful lot about my family.'

'Your father is a very newsworthy man,' he pointed out. 'And your mother was once a top model; tragedy is always worth printing when it hurts such beautiful people. It sort of evens things out for the rest of us,' he said without emotion. 'Makes us realise that even these so-called "beautiful people" can have it rough too.'

'I suppose so,' she acknowledged slowly. 'Do you think it was the divorce that killed my mother?'

He nodded. 'I would say it could have helped, wouldn't you?'

'But it was over six months ago!'

'I've heard that its never easy, and after almost twenty years together . . .'

'Yes,' she agreed dully. 'Although she seemed to have put her life back together so well.'

'Maybe she had, maybe it was something else that triggered her death.' The blue eyes probed.

Chelsea shook her head. 'Everything was the same as it always was.'

'Sure?'

'Well I can't be sure,' she answered regretfully. 'We lived pretty much our own lives.'

'Of course, you continued to live with your mother after the separation, didn't you?'

She nodded. 'But I saw almost as much of Jace as I would if he had still lived with us, Mom did too.'

'Was there any specific reason you preferred to live with your mother?'

'None at—Hey, why are you asking all these questions?' she frowned her chagrin.

His smile was instantaneous. 'Sorry. I just thought you needed to talk.'

Her own smile was rueful. 'Maybe I did, but I shouldn't burden a complete stranger with my family problems.'

'I don't mind.'

'But I do,' she said brightly. 'Why don't you tell me about yourself?'

He pulled a face. 'Because there isn't that much to tell.'

'Tell me anyway,' she invited interestedly.

He shrugged. 'I'm the only child of over-indulgent parents who don't understand me.'

Chelsea's grin was irrepressible. 'This story sounds very familiar!'

He raised mocking brows. 'Your parents don't understand you either?'

'No parents do when the child gets to a certain age. I think they would have to be as insane as us to understand the workings of a teenagers' mind!'

'Speak for yourself, I'm twenty-four,' he feigned indignation.

'Men develop later than women,' she teased.

'Not that much later,' John scoffed.

'So you don't live at home any more?' she prompted, relieved to have a change of subject from the last upsetting four days.

He shook his head. 'I moved out years ago.'

'Are you married?'

'Do I look married?' he scorned.

'No,' she laughed. 'But nowadays you just never know, looks can be deceiving.'

'Are *you* married?'

'You mean the newspapers didn't tell you that?' a trace of bitterness entered her voice.

'They mentioned an engagement.' There was a question in John's voice.

'It didn't work out,' she told him abruptly.

'Why not? I know,' he held up his hands defensively. 'I'm being inquisitive again. But I just wondered where Lucas McAdams fitted into the scheme of things.'

Her smile was mocking at the insinuation. 'As a friend of my parents, he certainly had nothing to do with my broken engagement; I doubt he even knew it existed!'

'Oh.'

'If you must know,' she sighed, 'Randy *was* immature for his age. He made a pass at my mother,' she explained irritably as she realised John still looked puzzled.

'Now that *was* immature,' John agreed with a disbelieving whistle.

'It was also stupid,' she said grimly, remembering her humiliation when her mother had had to tell her about Randy's attempt to get her into bed while he waited at the house for Chelsea to come home from work.

She and Randy had been together since

eleventh grade, and she had accepted his ring
only weeks after they had both left school. In the
two years they had dated they had been in and
out of each other's homes so much she had come
to regard his parents almost as her own; she had
thought he felt the same way about hers. Until
the day she came home from work to find her
mother in tears. She hadn't wanted to tell
Chelsea what was wrong at first, but finally she
had broken down completely and told her of
Randy's behaviour.

Chelsea had been stunned, even more hurt by
the fact that Randy denied it all. Somehow she
had felt it wouldn't have seemed so bad if he
could just have admitted to it. But even when she
had given him back his ring he had proclaimed
his innocence, and that she hadn't been able to
forgive.

'Very stupid,' she added disgustedly.

'Your mother was shocked, hm?'

'Of course she was shocked,' Chelsea snapped.
'Wouldn't you be?'

His mouth quirked with rueful humour. 'I
doubt it will ever happen to me!'

Some of the tension left her, her mouth
relaxing into a smile. 'No,' she acknowledged,
pushing thoughts of Randy's treachery from her
mind. 'Just another example of the bad luck of
one of the "beautiful people"?' she mocked.

'You were hurt very badly,' John sympathised
softly.

She shrugged. 'It's all part of growing up, I
guess,' she dismissed past pain.

'So Lucas is just a friend?'

'Of my father's,' Chelsea repeated, absently
stirring the now cold coffee round in the bottom
of her cup. 'But I knew him years ago too. How

come you don't know him when you live in the same building?'

'London can be like that,' he dismissed.

'Los Angeles too,' she sighed.

'Besides,' John added dryly, 'your Lucas isn't the easiest of men to get close to.'

'No,' she acknowledged thoughtfully. 'And he isn't *my* Lucas, a woman called Jennifer has that privilege.' Privilege? Did she really think it would be that to be Lucas's girlfriend?

'Jennifer Sutton,' he nodded.

Chelsea's eyes widened. 'You know her?'

'*Of* her,' he corrected. 'She works at your—at your *father's* friend's law-firm. It's been rumoured for months that he's going to make her a partner in the near future, perhaps in more than the law-firm.'

It didn't surprise her that Lucas was seeing a woman who shared his interest in the law as well as his sophistication and maturity. And maybe John was right, maybe the other couple would eventually marry, although she doubted it would be for love on Lucas's side; he certainly didn't talk or act like a man madly in love!

'An ideal marriage,' she said dryly.

'You sound sceptical,' John raised dark blond brows.

She shook her head. 'How can I be, I've never met Jennifer Sutton.'

'But you do know Lucas McAdams. Do you think she sounds the sort of woman who could make him happy?'

She pulled a face. 'Who knows?' she was non-committal, suddenly realising how much of her own personal life and those around her that she had revealed to this man. She glanced at her wristwatch, gasping as she realised she was already forty minutes late for having lunch with Lucas at his apartment. 'I didn't realise it was that late,' she chewed worriedly on her bottom lip. 'I'm sure I must have kept you from something too . . .?'

'Not at all,' he answered smoothly. 'I've enjoyed talking with you.'

'But you were going home when we met.'

'It was nothing important,' he shrugged dismissively.

'Well I have to be going now anyway.' She picked up her purse. 'I'm going to be very late for lunch with Lucas,' she grimaced.

'I hope I won't get you into trouble.' John stood up too, moving to pay the bill.

'I'm getting used to it.' She followed him outside once he had insisted on paying for the coffees. 'Lucas is a hard man to please.'

'I've heard that,' he nodded. 'So maybe you had better not tell him we spent the last couple of hours together.'

Chelsea frowned at that. 'He doesn't disapprove of you, too?'

'Too?' John prompted lightly.

She gave a rueful smile. 'I think he considers me to be a cross between Mata Hari and Alice in Wonderland!' she derided.

'Well you have the hair to play the latter part, but where does Mata Hari come into it?'

Her sense of humour had recovered quite a lot since yesterday, and she recounted the incident in the elevator with mischievous relish.

John's grin was appreciative. 'That was a momentous first meeting after so many years. I'm sure Lucas must have been embarrassed once he knew the truth.'

'That's an understatement,' she laughed, remembering Lucas's awkwardness.

'I'll bet.' John got out of the taxi-cab with her as they reached the apartment building. 'I'll leave you here, I have to get back to work now.'

She frowned her concern. 'I hope I haven't got you into trouble, we've been talking for hours.'

'I've enjoyed it.' He took her hand in his. 'Thanks.'

Chelsea shook her head. 'I should be the one thanking you, I was feeling down and you helped me feel a little better. I'm going to be in London for a few more weeks, so maybe we could meet again . . .?'

'Maybe we could,' John's reply was non-committal as he released her hands. 'You're sure to see me about.'

She was a little disappointed that he didn't want to make a definite date to see her again, but as he said, she was sure to see him about the building. And she couldn't really make any definite plans herself, not when her actions were mainly governed by Lucas's movements.

The thought of Lucas reminded her that he was probably impatiently waiting for her upstairs. 'I'd better go,' she said gratefully, having liked John immensely, not looking forward to entering the apartment that was Lucas's cold world. 'It was nice talking to you.'

'It was nice listening to you.'

'I've probably bored you half to death,' she realised ruefully. 'But thanks for being too polite to say so.'

She could feel her tension returning as the elevator ascended; Lucas was going to be far from pleased by her delay, especially when he had come home specifically to see her.

She waited several long minutes for Mrs Harvey to open the door to her, the woman's face disapproving when she did so. When was it anything else! She and Lucas made a good pair; maybe he should marry his housekeeper!

She was being ungrateful now. Neither Lucas or Mrs Harvey had expected—or wanted?—a nineteen-year-old guest. 'Sorry I'm late,' she smiled engagingly, walking through to the lounge. 'Where's Lucas?' she asked softly.

'Mr McAdams had to return to his office,' the housekeeper told her stiltedly. 'He waited until one o'clock, and when you still hadn't returned . . .'

'I see,' Chelsea grimaced. 'What sort of mood was he in when he left?'

'Mr McAdams was naturally very disappointed that you weren't here——'

'Don't say any more,' she shook her head. 'I can imagine the rest.' Mrs Harvey was too loyal to her employer to say that he had been furiously angry when he left. But Chelsea knew that he must have been, and in all honesty she knew he had a right to be. Her only excuse was that she had intended being back by twelve-thirty, she had just forgotten the time. But if Lucas disapproved of John he was unlikely to appreciate being told who had delayed her. Maybe she would take John's advice and not mention him to the other man.

'I've kept a lunch hot for you,' Mrs Harvey told her stiffly.

'You didn't have to do that,' she protested.

'If you'll just sit down in the dining-room I'll bring it through to you.'

Chelsea still had no appetite for food, but she would just be adding insult to injury if she refused the meal the housekeeper had prepared for her.

And in truth the food was delicious, chicken pie with a light pastry crust, succulent peas, and a baked potato, the gravy she poured over the meal the best she had ever tasted. Once Chelsea began to eat she realised how hungry she had really been, somehow managing to clear the plate, although she refused the fruit and ice-cream for dessert, not able to eat anything else.

'That was lovely, Mrs Harvey,' she told the other woman sincerely, standing up to help clear the table.

'I can do that.' The housekeeper took the plates out of her hands.

'I can help.' Chelsea picked up the condiment set and the glass that had contained her water and carried it through to the kitchen.

'But——'

'I don't want, or need, waiting on,' she told the older woman firmly. 'I realise its your job, and that you like to do these things for Lucas, but I would prefer to do my share of the work.'

The housekeeper looked at her stubbornly set mouth and steady blue eyes. 'Very well,' she finally conceded. 'Although I will continue to cook the meals.'

'Are you kidding!' Chelsea gave a mischievous grin. 'After the meal I've just eaten you won't get any arguments from me on that score.'

The woman's habitually stern expression relaxed slightly. 'I'm glad you enjoyed it,' she said almost shyly.

'It's the first thing I've been tempted to eat since——' she broke off emotionally.

'I'm glad,' Mrs Harvey said gently. 'Why don't you go and rest until its time for dinner; I'm sure you must be tired. You see,' she teased abruptly as Chelsea yawned as if on cue.

'Auto-suggestion,' she said dryly. 'Although I am a little tired.'

'I'll bring you a nice cup of tea before I leave at four,' the housekeeper told her softly. 'Unless you would prefer coffee?'

'I think I would, if you don't mind,' she nodded.

'I don't mind at all. Now off you go.' She was instructed firmly. 'I'll try not to disturb you.'

Chelsea yawned continuously as she stripped off ready for bed, but at least the housekeeper had thawed towards her a little. She could only hope Lucas would eventually do the same. Although after her absence lunch-time when he came home she had a feeling she was going to be in trouble when he returned tonight.

But John had been nice, so easy to talk to after Lucas's rigidity, that she hadn't really wanted to leave him. She hoped she did see him again; she really liked him.

It seemed as if she were no sooner falling asleep than Mrs Harvey was gently shaking her awake. 'Is it four o'clock already?' she asked groggily, pushing the cascade of silver hair from her face to look up at the other woman.

'It's only a little after three,' the housekeeper told her regretfully. 'Mr McAdams telephoned earlier, and I——'

'Was he still mad at me?'

'He didn't say,' Mrs Harvey dismissed. 'He just wanted to make sure you got home all right, and he told me not to disturb you when I explained you were sleeping. But I'm sure you will want to take this second telephone call.'

Chelsea frowned, getting out of bed to pull on her robe, suddenly realising she had embarrassed the other woman with her lack of clothing. 'Sorry,' she gave a rueful grimace. 'I think maybe I'd better buy myself some nightgowns.'

'I think that might be a good idea,' Mrs Harvey nodded. 'The telephone is in the lounge,' she told Chelsea as she left the room.

'It must be urgent for Lucas to ring again so soon after the last time——'

'It isn't Mr McAdams,' she shook her head.

'It isn't?' she frowned. 'Then who—Jace!' she said excitedly. 'Is it Jace?'

'I believe the man said he was your father——'

'That is Jace!' She grabbed up the receiver. 'Daddy!' she said emotionally.

'You haven't called me that since you were five years old,' came his gruff reply.

She gave a shaky laugh, smiling her thanks at Mrs Harvey as she tactfully left the room. 'And I probably won't call you it again for another fourteen years,' she warned. 'I forgot myself for a few minutes.'

'Don't apologise, I quite liked it. I called to see how you are, Princess,' he added seriously, sounding so far away, even though it was a very good line.

She had been his 'Princess' ever since she could remember, their relationship very warm and loving. 'I'm fine,' she told him steadily.

'Sure?'

'Sure,' she confirmed, knowing she did feel much better today, that sleep and food had helped put things back in perspective.

'All hell has broken loose over here,' he sighed tiredly. 'You haven't been bothered by the media at all?' he asked sharply.

'No,' she assured him, well able to imagine the pressure he was under. 'Don't worry about me.'

'All right, Princess,' he said with some relief. 'I've been trying to reach Lucas all day, but somehow I keep missing him, both there and at his office.'

'He should be home by about six-o'clock English time.'

'I'll call him if I get the chance,' Jace told her. 'How are things going between the two of you?'

'Fine—once I'd convinced him of who I was,' she said dryly, going on to explain Lucas's absence from home the last few days, although she omitted to tell Jace about the confusion in the elevator before Lucas became convinced of her identity; her father had enough to worry about without her telling him his friend had assumed his daughter was a hooker! 'Everything is okay now,' she assured him. 'And I know Lucas does want to talk to you. How are you coping?' she asked huskily.

'You know me,' he dismissed lightly.

Yes, she did. And she knew that even though her parents were divorced that there had still been a lot of affection between them; Jace was probably hurting almost as badly as she was. Almost. But he couldn't know the same guilt that consumed her.

'Is Camilla still helping out?' At least if she knew the other woman was with him she wouldn't worry about him quite so much.

'She's—around,' he answered vaguely. 'You know Camilla. Now I'd better let you get back to sleep, I'll call and talk to you in a few days.'

'Maybe, if Lucas doesn't mind, I could call you.'

'I'm sure he won't,' Jace dismissed. 'But I won't be at the apartment, too many people know that address. I'll telephone you once I've found somewhere more—private, to stay.'

'I love you,' she told him softly.

'I love you too, Princess,' his voice was husky.

Her expression was thoughtful as she turned from replacing the receiver. She could well imagine the hounding Jace was getting from the media. Maybe it was the price he paid for being one of those so-called 'beautiful people', as John had said, but that didn't make it any easier.

'Would you like that coffee now?' Mrs Harvey offered gently, standing in the kitchen doorway.

Chelsea forced herself to smile. 'Yes, please,' she said gratefully. 'I'm fully awake now, so I may as well get up.'

She was just pulling a navy blue blouse on over her bared breasts when the gentle thud on the bedroom door alerted her to the housekeeper's presence. 'You didn't have to——' her smile faded somewhat as she saw Mrs Harvey wasn't bringing her the coffee at all, that she carried several large boxes into the room and deposited them on the bed. 'What on earth . . .!'

'From Mr McAdams,' the housekeeper smiled. 'The label on the boxes is that of a well-known lingerie shop. Wasn't that kind of him?'

Chelsea was well aware of the fame of the establishment named on the boxes, she also knew Lucas hadn't made the gesture out of kindness. With the gift he intended making certain last night's incident didn't happen again. She couldn't take the nightgowns, but nevertheless, her fingers itched to see what Lucas's taste was in women's nightwear.

'Very kind,' she answered Mrs Harvey, not intending to upset her tenuous relationship with the other woman by telling her she couldn't accept the 'kind' gesture. 'Shall we have a look inside?' she invited mischievously, opening the top box, echoing Mrs Harvey's gasp at the beauty of the frivolously lacy garment the folding back of the tissue-paper revealed, its colour pure ivory, knowing that it would look beautiful against her pale skin and silver hair.

The other two boxes revealed nightgowns equally as beautiful and feminine, one of peach lace, the other the palest lemon Chelsea had ever seen. Lucas had *beautiful* taste in women's nightwear, so much so that she decided to give him the money for them rather than return them as she had at first planned to do; she couldn't have chosen better herself, if she had to wear a nightgown.

'They're lovely,' Mrs Harvey echoed her feelings.

'Exquisite.' She hung the three lacy garments in the wardrobe with her other clothes. 'Lucas has a wonderful eye for colour.'

'Oh I'm sure Mr McAdams wouldn't have chosen the gowns himself,' the housekeeper sounded shocked at the assumption that he would have done. 'He would simply have telephoned the shop, given them a description of your colouring, and left it to their discretion.'

She had a feeling the other woman was right, and somehow that knowledge took away some of the pleasure of the gift, made it seem impersonal, more just a need to remind her that he didn't want a repeat of the previous night.

'Then the saleswoman has an eye for colour,' she said brightly, picking up the empty boxes. 'I may as well join you in the kitchen for that coffee.'

Much as she was coming to like the other woman, Mrs Harvey having thawed considerably towards her as the day progressed, she was still glad of the time alone once the housekeeper had left for the day, the instructions for the already prepared dinner written down in the kitchen; Chelsea was determined to be the one to do those last-minute preparations.

Mrs Harvey had told her that Lucas usually wore something casual when he dined at home, and deciding her denims and blouse were too casual she went to her bedroom shortly before six to change into a high-necked navy blue dress, a sash-belt at her narrow waist, her tights also navy blue, as were her high heeled sandals. Her hair flowed long and silky to her waist, her make-up light; she was going to need all the self-confidence she had to face Lucas after the last occasion he had seen her!

She was waiting in the lounge with the whisky and the dash of water already poured into a glass that Mrs Harvey had told her was Lucas's usual drink when he came in. He hadn't seen her as he put his briefcase down on the hall table, lines of weariness etched beside his eyes and mouth, although he looked just as dark and virile in the dark grey three-piece suit as he usually did.

His eyes narrowed as he looked up and saw her standing proudly in front of the window, the dark brown curtains a perfect foil for her silver-blonde hair.

'Hi,' she greeted huskily, walking across the room to hand him the prepared drink. 'Mrs Harvey told me your preference,' she explained at his questioning look.

He took a large swallow of the whisky and water. 'It's good,' he admitted grudgingly.

As she had taken such care with it she was glad about that! 'Have you had a hard day?' she asked politely. 'You look tired.'

He flexed his stiff shoulder muscles. 'I am tired. But don't feel you have to do this just because you're my guest.' His mouth twisted.

Chelsea frowned. 'Do what?'

'Welcome me home with the customary drink,' he grimaced. 'And then dutifully ask me about my day. I can assure you I've survived for thirty-four years without such solicitations, I can manage without it now!'

She blushed at his derision. 'I was genuinely interested,' she snapped. 'But if you don't want to talk to me that's okay! Dinner will be ready in twenty minutes, I hope that's long enough for you.'

'Chelsea!' he impatiently halted her angry exit from the room.

Tears glistened in her eyes as she faced him. 'Yes?' she asked defensively.

He sighed, his mouth compressed tightly. 'I'm sorry,' he said quietly. 'It's been a hell of a day but I had no right to take it out on you. And twenty minutes is quite long enough for me to shower and change,' he added gently.

She relaxed a little as she went into the kitchen, although she was very much aware that they had yet to touch on the sensitive subject of her sleepwalking, and the nightgowns that had been delivered because of it. That could cause even more tension between them.

She had the tureen of soup on the table when Lucas rejoined her, her breath catching in her throat at his casually attractive appearance, the dark brown of his shirt the same chocolate colour of his eyes, fitted tautly across his chest and flat stomach, beige slacks moulded to his muscular thighs and legs.

'It smells good.' Lucas seemed determined to be friendly as he sat down opposite her.

'I'm sure it will be if its as good as lunch,' she nodded. 'Er—I'm sorry about that, that I missed you I mean,' she was making a terrible job of apologising. 'I went out and then forgot the time.'

The tension had returned to his lean body. 'Did you go anywhere interesting?'

She knew what he was really asking, and she shrugged dismissively. 'Just for a walk and a cup of coffee.' She didn't mention the fact that she had had a companion.

'I see.' He didn't sound impressed with her explanation.

'Jace called,' she told him abruptly as she served the roast beef and accompanying vegetables.

'When?' Lucas rasped.

She shrugged. 'Just after you did, apparently.'

'You spoke to him?'

'Yes.' She frowned at his harshness.

'Is—everything, all right?'

'Well he's had to move out of his apartment temporarily because of the publicity,' she shrugged. 'But other than that he said everything was fine.'

'Damn,' Lucas muttered. 'I'm sorry I missed him, I've been trying to reach him all day.'

She nodded. 'He's been trying to reach you too.'

Lucas's eyes narrowed. 'Did he say why?'

'Just to talk, I think. He said he would call again when things have calmed down a little.'

'And Camilla, did he mention her?' Lucas rasped.

Chelsea frowned at his renewed tension. 'He said she was still helping him.'

'Good,' he bit out with satisfaction.

'Er—Lucas,' she paused hesitantly as he pinpointed her with icy brown eyes. 'The—the nightgowns arrived this afternoon.' She took the safest route to the subject she really wanted to talk about; her nudity last night!

His expression became even more remote. 'I trust they were the right size.'

She nodded. 'I'd like the bill so that I can pay you for them.'

'They're a gift,' he refused with arrogance.

'I'd rather pay for them myself,' she told him with dignity.

'And I said it isn't necessary,' he dismissed haughtily, continuing with his meal as if that were the end of the subject.

'Of course it is,' she snapped, wondering how anyone ever got through to this man. 'We both know the reason you purchased them, and it isn't your responsibility that I chose to wander around the apartment stark naked!' There, she had finally mentioned the embarrassing incident.

Except for a further tightening of his mouth Lucas showed no emotion on the subject. 'You didn't choose to do it, you were emotionally disturbed.'

Chelsea gave him an exasperated glare. 'I was also naked!' she said again.

He sighed, obviously impatient at not being able to relax and enjoy his fast cooling meal. 'I did notice that fact,' he drawled derisively.

'And it didn't bother you?' she snapped her resentment at this easy dismissal of her.

'I understood the reason for your sleepwalking——'

'Did you?' she interrupted shrilly. 'Did you really?' she accused heatedly.

Lucas looked at her with controlled eyes. 'Of

course.' His patience was one of boredom now.

It was his calmness and boredom that pushed her over the edge of being merely indignant at his dismissal of her nudity into a burning anger. How dare he dismiss her as if she were a child, with the body of one!

'How could you possibly understand my feelings?' she stood up in her agitation. 'How can anyone who hasn't suffered the same experience understand the numbing shock of having your mother take her own life!'

CHAPTER FOUR

THE stunned silence that followed Chelsea's outburst gave her enough time to realise exactly what she had said, and who she had said it to.

She had known when she found her mother unconscious that she hadn't suffered a heart-attack, her expression too peaceful and serene for that, the empty bottle of pills on the bedside table damning evidence of what had really happened. But from the moment Jace arrived on the scene everyone, from the doctor on down, had called it heart-failure. They were protecting her for her father's sake, at his request, she knew that, and she loved him for it, but living with the lie, having to pretend she didn't know the truth, was breaking her up inside.

And Lucas looked so dismayed by what she had said in the heat of her anger that she knew he had been protecting her from the truth too.

'I'm sorry,' she choked, turning on her heel to run to her bedroom, all the time remembering the nightmare of knowing her mother, her beautiful mother, had cared so little for her life, for the life they had together, that she had chosen to die rather than continue it. She hadn't even left them a note, had just taken the pills, lain down in the bed, and slowly died.

And she had been alone. If only Chelsea had come home as planned, maybe she could have talked her mother out of whatever depression had claimed her. But their lives had taken such different courses lately, their conversations only surface deep; she still had no idea what had driven her mother to kill herself. The divorce had been quite amiable, and was so long ago that she couldn't agree with John's suggestion that it had been that. John had known of her mother's suicide, of course, had been allowed to see the newspapers Lucas had been protecting her from all day, had read of the intimacy of their private lives.

Admittedly her mother hadn't dated at all since the divorce, but she had enjoyed her career, had recently become the top realtor in their area. And she had seemed to enjoy life. So the question remained *why*? Why would a beautiful thirty-nine-year-old woman, surrounded by people who loved and cared for her, contemplate suicide, let alone go through with it? Chelsea didn't have any of the answers, and that hurt almost as much as knowing she could perhaps have prevented it happening.

'You knew all the time that your mother's death was suicide?'

She turned slowly at the gruffly voiced question, Lucas standing in the open doorway to her bedroom. 'Yes, I knew,' she admitted dully.

'Jace doesn't think that you do.' He came completely into the room, sitting down on the single bed she had slept in the night before.

She shrugged, swallowing hard. 'I realise that. I—He didn't seem to want me to know either, so I went along with the heart-failure story.'

'And coming here.'

She chewed on her bottom lip, her hands laced tightly together. 'It was what he wanted.'

'Yes,' Lucas nodded. 'And even though you know the truth I still think he was right to do so.'

'Perhaps. Although it could have been something we shared together.'

Lucas's mouth twisted. 'Jace still thinks of you as his little Princess!'

'I know that,' she sighed. 'But I'm all grown up now, and able to take the truth, no matter what it might be, or how painful it is.'

'The Princess has left her ivory tower?' he taunted.

'I left it a long time ago, if anyone had cared to notice!' she snapped. 'But no one did.'

'It's called love, Chelsea,' he rasped. 'You should feel privileged to be surrounded by such love. Some of us haven't been so lucky in our parents.'

'But your mother and father were wonderful to you and Camilla.' She frowned at the bitterness in his voice.

He shook his head. 'They built us in their own image and were disappointed with the result,' he rasped. 'You were too young seven years ago to see that, but Camilla was frivolous and shallow to enter modelling, and I could never be as good a lawyer as my father! You've never been able to do a thing wrong in your parents' eyes since the day you were born, so don't blame Jace for trying to protect you still. It's done out of love!' Lucas bit out.

She blushed at the rebuke. 'I never realised . . . I thought you and Camilla had a happy childhood,' she admitted. 'Camilla doesn't seem to have been affected by the way it really was.'

'Meaning I have?' he grated.

'I didn't mean that. I—Yes, I did,' she grimaced, at last knowing the reason for his coldness. It wasn't an unhappy affair at all but his strict upbringing with intolerant parents had made him the coldly harsh man he was now. 'You were always very serious, Lucas, but now you're——'

'I don't care to discuss my character deficiencies,' he cut in harshly. 'We seem to have got off the subject, and that was your mother's suicide. How are you handling it?'

Her mouth twisted. 'By walking around the apartment naked! So much for our agreement that I would dress respectably outside the privacy of my bedroom!' she said self-derisively.

He gave an arrogant inclination of his head, the overhead lighting picking up several strands of grey among the darkness of his hair. 'We've already solved that problem,' he dismissed.

'I don't think we *solved* it at all,' she told him sharply. 'I want to pay for the nightgowns, and you refuse to let me.'

'Surely the matter is too trivial to argue about?' he scorned.

'Not to me! And I'm sure Jace doesn't expect you to give me expensive gifts either.'

'I'm sure Jace doesn't realise you sleep in the nude!' came back the impatient reply.

'Yes, he does,' she snapped.

Lucas frowned. 'He approves?'

'Why shouldn't he?' she shrugged. 'There's nothing shameful about the human body.'

His mouth tightened, a pulse beating in the rigidity of his jaw. 'No, there isn't,' he acknowledged tautly, the dark brown eyes emotionless.

Chelsea looked at him closely, noticing the white line of tension about his mouth, his hands clenched into fists at his sides. 'What's the matter, Lucas,' she taunted. 'Did you like what you saw?'

He looked at her with cold disdain. 'I don't believe we should be having this conversation!'

'Why not? Do you think of me as a child too, Lucas?' her voice had lowered huskily. She had no idea why she was doing this, but it suddenly seemed very important that she elicit some response from Lucas, even if it were only anger.

'No,' he rasped. 'I know you aren't.'

'Do you?' she breathed softly. 'How?'

His mouth tightened ominously, his eyes icy. 'What do you want from me, Chelsea?'

'The truth,' she sighed heavily. 'Something no one seems inclined to give me at the moment.'

'Then I will,' he ground out. 'I woke in the night because I heard a noise, I left my bedroom expecting to find a burglar at least. What I saw was——' he broke off abruptly, reluctant to go on.

'Yes?' she prompted, the tension in the room almost at breaking point.

'At first the figure seemed almost ghostly,' he continued grimly. 'Long silver hair, almost white in the moonlight, a pure white body. And then it took on the distinct shape of a woman,' he grated. 'A tall, slender woman with high thrusting breasts, a waist so slender I could have spanned it with my two hands, gently curving thighs and hips, their beauty begging to be touched, and legs so long and shapely they seemed never to end. Even the feet were perfect!' he finished harshly.

Chelsea was breathing erratically, shaken by his description of her. 'That was poetic, Lucas,' she gasped breathlessly.

His gaze raked over her insultingly. 'Don't mistake me for some simpering idiot, because I'm very much a man,' he rasped. 'And if you ever goad me like this again you could find yourself facing more than you're prepared to know. Do I make myself clear?' he bit out precisely.

The mood of intimacy was broken with his harsh rebuke, and Chelsea flushed guiltily. What was she *doing*! Lucas was a family friend, more of her father's than her own really, and for a few brief moments she *had* been goading him, had wanted—something. She wasn't even sure herself what that something had been, oblivion perhaps. And she knew Lucas could give her that. A few moments ago he had given her an insight into his sensuality that had surprised, as well as excited, her.

'I'm sorry,' she told him softly, her eyes pleading for his understanding.

His expression softened a little. 'Your apology is accepted. Now will you come and finish your dinner?' he encouraged softly.

She shook her head. 'I'm not hungry.'

'Then come and talk to me,' he suggested softly.

Her eyes widened. 'You aren't going out tonight?'

'I didn't go out yesterday evening in the end,' he told her. 'I cancelled my dinner engagement.'

'Because of me,' she sighed.

'Because I wouldn't have felt comfortable leaving you alone here,' he corrected.

'That must have made me even more popular with Jennifer,' she grimaced.

'She understood,' he dismissed arrogantly. 'I've invited her over to dinner tomorrow evening so that the two of you can meet.'

The thought of being 'looked over' by Lucas's mistress didn't exactly thrill her, but for the sake of the few weeks she was going to be here she knew she didn't have the right to upset his relationship with the other woman. 'That will be nice,' she answered flatly. 'Do you think the two of us will get on well together?'

'Does it matter?' he dismissed.

'No, I suppose not,' she sighed. 'I'll be okay this evening on my own if you want to go and see her.'

'I don't,' he stated haughtily. 'I told you, it's been a long and tiring day,' he reminded as they entered the lounge together, Lucas moving to pour them both a drink.

'I thought that sort of thing was supposed to relax you,' she dared to tease.

'Don't you know?' he mocked.

'Little Ol' Innocent me?' she pretended to be shocked.

'Yes.' The semblence of a smile softened the sternness of his mouth, and in that moment Chelsea determined to make him laugh, really laugh, before she returned to the States. It wasn't right that any human being should have so little laughter in his life, and if Lucas would only lighten up he——

Yes, he what? He was attractive now, but if he would only relax and enjoy life a little more he would be devastating!

'I have no idea,' she told him truthfully.

'But you were engaged for a while, weren't you? I thought that gave you licence to do anything you wanted nowadays?' He handed her a glass, sitting down opposite her, his long legs stretched out in front of him as he relaxed.

'Randy and I had been friends since High School,' she shrugged. 'I don't know, I guess we just didn't think about making love.'

'Isn't that a little strange?'

'Maybe,' she conceded with a frown. She and

Randy had been so busy having fun, sharing a lot of athletic activities with their friends, that it hadn't occurred to either of them that they should be taking every opportunity they could to jump into bed together. Maybe her ignorance, her disinclination, had been the reason Randy had made a pass at her mother. 'But we didn't,' she frowned.

'Well "that sort of thing" *is* supposed to help relax you,' Lucas drawled softly. 'And most of the time it does. But Jennifer is a very social woman, and I don't feel in the mood to go to a party before we can go to bed.'

Her eyes widened. 'You can be very forthright, when you want to be, can't you?'

'I thought that was what you wanted from me?'

'I do. I just——'

'Don't tell me I've succeeded in shocking you, Chelsea?' he mocked.

'I—Of course not,' she dismissed with more nonchalance than she felt.

'Liar!' he taunted.

'Did you do it on purpose?' she frowned.

'Well, you aren't the only one with shock value, you know,' he mused.

'You did do it on purpose,' she looked at him with new eyes. 'I bet you're lethal in a court-room!'

'So they tell me,' he nodded, sipping his drink.

Chelsea tried her own drink, surprised to find it was the Scotch and coke that she liked, exactly as she liked it. 'How much *did* Jace tell you in that cable?'

'Certainly not your preference in drinks,' Lucas laughed softly. 'No, I remembered that from something else he once told me.'

'I can't think what?' she frowned, somehow

disconcerted by the fact that Jace seemed to have talked to this man about her when she knew nothing about this Lucas other than what she had learnt the last two days.

'It seems that last year you went to the expense of buying him a twenty-year-old bottle of Scotch for Christmas, and then proceeded to drink half of it for him by drowning it with Coke. Any man with a sense of values would have to be disgusted by such an action,' he taunted. 'It's sacrilege!'

She met the laughter in his eyes with a rueful grin. 'Neat Scotch tastes awful.'

'Not when it's twenty years old!' Lucas shook his head.

'Any neat Scotch,' she insisted.

'I bet you also close your eyes on a Roller Coaster,' Lucas mocked.

'Isn't that the same as closing your eyes when you make love?' she asked guilelessly.

'So we're back to that,' he derided. 'Wait until you have some experience of your own and then we can discuss it.'

'Very neatly avoided,' she laughed softly.

'It's called evasive tactics,' he almost smiled with her.

'A legal term?'

'A self-protective one,' he drawled. 'Would you like to put a record on the stereo?' he invited, standing up to show her a cupboard that contained an extensive collection of records and cassettes. 'Some of them are Camilla's,' he added mockingly. 'So you should find something in there that you like.'

'You don't have a television?' she ignored the taunt, looking through the cassettes.

'A socially destructive machine,' he stated with his usual arrogance.

'Yes,' she nodded.

'You agree?'

'Sure,' she pulled out a Barbra Streisand cassette. 'Did you see her latest movie?' she asked as she deftly put the cassette on.

He shook his head. 'I very rarely find the time to go to the cinema.'

Chelsea nodded, not able somehow to imagine his settling down with a tub of caramel popcorn and a Coke while he watched a two-or three-hour movie. 'The critics were undecided, but Mom and I——' she broke off, pain flickering across her face.

'It never hurts to remember the good times, Chelsea,' Lucas encouraged gently.

'We had a good time,' she continued determinedly as the silky voice of the famous actress–singer filled the room. 'It was worth going just to see her sing.'

To say she and Lucas spent a pleasant evening together would perhaps be going a little too far, there were too many awkward silences for that, but when she made her way to her bedroom just over an hour later Chelsea could say in all honesty that they had progressed towards an uneasy friendship tonight, that they may even reach a complete one before she left. She hoped that they would.

And she didn't have to pretend with Lucas anymore, could show him the pain her mother's suicide gave her without having to hide behind the truth as she did with Jace. Having the truth between them gave Lucas and herself a bond that sat strangely between them.

'You stupid little idiot!'

Chelsea came awake with a startled jerk,

staring up at Lucas, a beige silk robe over his pyjamas, in stunned surprise. Whatever tenuous friendship they had reached last night was wiped out by the furious anger in Lucas's harsh face as he towered over her.

'I—What is it?' she sat up, blinking at him dazedly, looking very young with her make-upless face and her hair confined at her nape. 'What time is it?'

'Just after seven,' he rasped. 'Someone very kindly delivered this outside the door before disappearing!' He threw down the newspaper that he held in his hand down on to her bed.

Chelsea still blinked foggily. 'I don't understand.'

'You will after you've read that,' Lucas ground out.

She grimaced. 'I don't think I can even see it, let alone read it!' she said ruefully.

'This is no time for levity,' he growled with angry impatience. 'Read the story on the front cover.'

'Can I brush my teeth first?' Her mouth felt awful!

'No!'

She flinched at the fury he projected in that one word; so much for thinking they might be becoming friends!

She straightened in the bed to lean back against the headboard, wearing the ivory coloured nightgown, the lacy cups over her breasts revealing her darkened nipples, her skin palely transluscent against its delicacy. But she forgot her own appearance as a photograph of herself appeared on the front cover of the newspaper, the story accompanying the photograph getting worse and worse as she read on.

'Oh no,' she cringed. 'Oh no!' she gasped. 'Oh *no*,' she groaned her embarrassment.

'I think, with the evidence in your own hands, that we can safely assume, oh yes!' Lucas bit out impatiently, having been pacing the room as she read.

Chelsea could now understand his blazing anger. The story clearly stated that the daughter of Gloria and Jace Stevens was staying at the apartment of eligible bachelor Lucas McAdams, that he was reputed to be 'an old friend of the family'—and the innuendo behind that was enough to make her cringe! It also said that she had flown to England to be with Lucas as soon as her mother's funeral was over. It then went on to detail her mother's death and the speculation attached to that, ending with a query as to what Lucas McAdam's long-time companion Jennifer Sutton thought of him having the beautiful Chelsea Stevens in residence with her lover.

It was a terrible story, one that concentrated more on conjecture and innuendo about herself and Lucas than it did on the terrible tragedy of her mother's death.

'It's awful.' She pushed the newspaper away disgustedly.

'But it's basically accurate,' Lucas said grimly.

'Basically,' she agreed contemptuously. 'But the facts have been embroidered out of recognition.'

'And just how do you think this particular reporter got hold of the "facts"?'

She shrugged. 'I have no idea. I suppose——' she broke off, frowning deeply. 'Why are you looking at me like that?' she asked slowly, not liking the condemning expression in his eyes at all.

'I called the newspaper as soon as I'd read the story,' Lucas bit out with icy precision, as if he wanted there to be no misunderstanding about what he was saying. 'They told me that their informant was a man called John Anderson. Ring any bells?' he asked softly.

Chelsea had gone paper-white at the mention of John's name. 'But he—He isn't a reporter,' she protested weakly. 'He lives here!'

Lucas shook his head. 'I have no idea where he lives, but it certainly isn't here!'

She closed her eyes in denial of her own stupidity. John hadn't actually said that he lived in this apartment building, only that he had been on his way up to the eighth floor, and that he knew Lucas lived there. She realised now that he must have been looking for her, and that by some quirk of fate she had stepped in the lift as he was arriving.

'I didn't realise,' she groaned. 'He was so nice, and so—so easy to talk to.'

'Obviously!' Lucas said disgustedly.

'You don't think I actually told him this garbage?'

'You told him enough,' Lucas grated.

Tears glistened in her dark blue eyes. 'I'm sorry,' she choked.

He glared at her. 'Being sorry isn't going to help this situation at all. I've already had to take the receiver off the hook to stop the calls from other newspapers. Thank God I've been able to stop them actually coming into the building!'

'How did you do that?'

'It's private, as I'm sure I've told you at least once before,' he said with heavy sarcasm. 'If any more reporters attempt to come up here I'll have them arrested!'

He would too, she could tell that by the implacability of his mouth.

'I'd sue the damned newspaper if I could,' he continued grimly. 'But unfortunately they printed nothing but the truth. And that truth was freely given to them!'

Her bottom lip quivered precariously. 'I've said I'm sorry. I had no idea John was a reporter.'

Lucas's eyes narrowed. 'Just how did you actually come to meet him and reveal so much?'

The embarrassed colour was a fixture in her cheeks by the time she had explained the meeting and how she had found it easy to talk to the other man. Of course she had found it easy to talk to him, it was his job to *make* it easy. She mentally winced as she remembered all the questions he had asked—and that she had answered. She may have been innocent in her confidences, but she should have had more sense than to talk to a stranger in that way. Lucas obviously thought so too.

'Why didn't you tell me about the meeting?' he demanded to know.

She swallowed hard. 'John said you didn't approve of him,' she revealed reluctantly.

'He's right, I don't!'

'I assumed he lived here and had done something to upset you. I realise now that he didn't want me to tell you and give you time to stop the story,' she said miserably.

'I doubt I could have done that,' Lucas rasped. 'But I might have been able to set his editor straight on a few of those so-called facts.'

'I really am sorry, Lucas,' she looked at him appealingly. 'I don't know what else I can say.'

'I think, in future,' he bit out coldly, 'it might

be better if you said as little as possible—to everyone.' He stormed out of the room.

That she had made Lucas furiously angry, and with good reason, she didn't doubt, that she had made an absolute fool of herself she didn't doubt either. A child would have seen through John's questioning, and yet she had gone ahead and told him things about herself she had told no one else. Although surprisingly John didn't seem to have written everything she had revealed to him, had omitted the reason for her broken engagement for one thing.

But something else was worrying her at the moment, something she had to talk to Lucas about immediately.

He was wearing only a brief towel wrapped about his hips when she entered his bedroom after the briefest of knocks, his mouth tightening at her intrusion.

'I don't remember telling you to come in,' he rasped.

'I thought you did.' She looked away awkwardly. 'I—I just wanted to ask you, will Jace get to see the article?' God, Lucas was magnificent when he was undressed! The conservative suits and shirts he wore went a long way to hiding just how broadly muscular he was, a fine sprinkling of hair covering his chest, thickening over his navel and down beneath the towel, his long legs covered in the same fine hair. And there was no way he could look coldly remote, dressed—or undressed—as he was now! He was blatantly masculine, his ruffled dark hair giving him a rakish appeal.

'It's possible,' he answered her. 'But I doubt it, not when it's an English newspaper. Why?' His eyes were narrowed.

'Because it's obvious from what they've written that I know my mother didn't die from natural causes.'

'It's unlikely that Jace will get to see it—or hear of it,' Lucas relented a little in his own anger to comfort her on that score. 'Although he's going to have to realise some day that you know.'

She nodded abruptly. 'That all I wanted to know, I'm sorry I bothered you.'

'Yes,' he acknowledged tersely. 'And, Chelsea,' he stopped her at the door, 'I shouldn't leave the apartment today,' he warned.

She flushed. 'Don't worry, I've learnt my lesson; I won't talk to any more amiable strangers.'

'That wasn't the reason I said it,' he shook his head. 'There are sure to be reporters outside most of the day, I wouldn't advise you to try and get past them.'

'No,' she agreed heavily. 'I—Will Miss Sutton still be coming to dinner this evening now?'

'I doubt she would miss it for anything,' he derided hardly. 'That should give the press even more reason for speculation,' he added grimly.

Chelsea nodded. 'I'll see you both this evening, then.' Her head was bent as she left the room, lost in her own thoughts, looking up with a guilty start as someone cleared their throat noisily. 'Mrs Harvey, you startled me!' She gave a bright smile.

'Indeed?' the frosty manner was back with a vengeance.

And no wonder, if the other woman had just seen her leaving Lucas's bedroom! Yesterday she had seen her returning his pyjama jacket, today she had actually seen her leaving Lucas's bedroom at seven-thirty in the morning wearing one of the sheer nightgowns he had purchased for her! It must all look very damning.

'I—er—I just went to talk to Lucas about something . . .' even to her own ears her excuse sounded lame, and Mrs Harvey obviously didn't believe a word!

'Is there anything special I can get you for breakfast?' the other woman asked coldly.

'I——'

'Chelsea, I——' The expression on Lucas's face as he stood in his bedroom doorway wearing only the towel was a sight to see as he took in the presence of his housekeeper, the disapproval on her tight-lipped face obvious. 'Good morning, Mrs Harvey,' he recovered quickly. 'I didn't realise you had arrived yet.'

The housekeeper's knowing expression seemed to say she realised that! 'I'm just about to cook breakfast,' she told him abruptly. 'I'll be in the kitchen if you need me.' Her expression said she clearly doubted that!

Chelsea looked at Lucas with wary eyes as the other woman's ramrod back disappeared in the direction of the kitchen. After all, she had been the cause of yet another embarrassment to him.

'I—You——' he seemed to be having trouble articulating, shaking his head ruefully. 'I can't believe this is happening to me,' he finally groaned.

'I——'

'For God's sake don't say you're sorry again!'

'I'm not sorry?' she grimaced.

His mouth quirked as he began to smile, the smile turning to full-blooded laughter. 'You're amazing, do you know that?' he chuckled.

She grinned back at him. 'I am?'

He nodded, completely relaxed, the anger she had been expecting at this latest situation she had created not materialising as he continued to smile, his husky laughter having left his eyes a warm brown. 'Since you arrived my life has been anything but dull. And now I think Mrs Harvey may resign because of you.'

He didn't sound particularly concerned considering how invaluable he had claimed her to be Chelsea's first evening here. 'Do you really think she will?' she frowned, having come to like the other woman; she certainly wouldn't want Mrs Harvey to give up a good job that she obviously liked just because of a misunderstanding.

Lucas shrugged unconcernedly. 'I doubt it. But you've certainly shaken my household up since you arrived here. Maybe I should keep you around all the time,' he added softly.

The atmosphere had suddenly changed between them, become suddenly still, tense with an emotion Chelsea couldn't fathom. But she did know she couldn't break away from the warmth of Lucas's eyes, or the way a nerve pulsed in his throat. And he seemed equally as mesmerised, their gazes locked and unlockable.

The tension became unbearable as the moments passed, until finally Chelsea could stand it no longer, shaking her head. 'Just for entertainment value, of course,' she attempted to tease, her hands feeling clammy from the exchange, her heart seeming to beat at twice it's normal rate.

Lucas seemed to pull out of the mood of intimacy that had surrounded them, with effort too, his mouth tightening self-critically. 'Of course,' he answered abruptly. 'You had better go and dress before breakfast,' he suggested curtly.

'And you,' she nodded, reluctant to move, wishing she hadn't broken that mood, wanting that closeness back again.

But Lucas was already going back into his bedroom and closing the door. Chelsea's own movements were slower. The morning had started out so badly, was a total disaster in fact, and yet now she felt good about it, had a warmth inside her that she couldn't seem to place, a warmth that had begun with Lucas's laughter.

She had managed to make him laugh, as she had promised herself she would, although not quite in the way she had thought she would. But Lucas had one of those rare humours that was worth waiting for, a laugh that made those about him feel good too. Yes, it had definitely been worth waiting for.

And somehow the thought of having to meet his mistress tonight didn't please her at all.

CHAPTER FIVE

SHE was in her room changing for dinner when she heard Lucas arrive home from work, later this evening, the time shortly before seven o'clock.

As Lucas had suggested she had spent a quiet day in the apartment, hadn't ventured out at all, Mrs Harvey confirming when she went out shopping mid-morning that there were several reporters and cameramen waiting outside. The housekeeper had been most disgusted that they had actually tried to question her.

Lucas had telephoned in the afternoon to make sure everything was all right, sounding like the lawyer once more, although now Chelsea had seen the softer side of him she didn't feel quite so in awe of him.

Remembering what little she had heard of Jennifer Sutton she chose her gown for the evening with that in mind. She never wore the colour black as it made her hair look brassy and false, the dark grey dress she chose making her hair appear more silver than ever, its close-fitting style emphasising the thrust of her breasts, shaped to her narrow waist to fall in gentle folds to just below her knees, her legs long and shapely, her height added to by sandals the same colour grey as her dress. She knew she looked attractive, older than her nineteen years, and that was the way she wanted it to be.

Mrs Harvey had taken the afternoon off so that she could prepare and serve the dinner, a usual

occurrence at any formal dinner Lucas gave,
apparently, and Chelsea went in to the kitchen to
watch the other woman once she was dressed,
Lucas still in his room. Things had been a little
strained between her and the housekeeper since
the incident outside Lucas's bedroom, although
the older woman was still polite.

'The fresh salmon looks delicious,' Chelsea
told her warmly, her mouth watering at the sight
of the three appetisers laying so temptingly on the
plate.

'It's Miss Sutton's favourite,' she was informed
stiltedly.

'Oh.'

'And Mr McAdams,' the housekeeper relented
slightly at her crestfallen expression.

'Does Miss Sutton eat here a lot?' she asked
with casual indifference.

'Once or twice a month,' Mrs Harvey dismissed.

That didn't sound such a lot, although that
didn't mean Lucas didn't spend all the other
evenings of the month eating out with Jennifer
Sutton or at her apartment.

'Is she beautiful?' Chelsea felt tempted to
ask.

Dark brows were raised disapprovingly over
light blue eyes. '"Beauty is in the eye of the
beholder",' Mrs Harvey quoted primly.

Chelsea's expression became mischievous. 'And
how does Miss Sutton "behold"?'

The older woman's expression softened
slightly. 'Very well,' she admitted ruefully.

'Blonde, or brunette, or neither?'

'A redhead,' the housekeeper confirmed.

'With a temper to match?'

She stiffened. 'I don't think I should be

discussing Mr McAdams's guest in this way.' She straightened as the doorbell rang. 'That will be Miss Sutton now.'

Chelsea tensed, smoothing down her dress with unsteady hands. 'Yes,' she acknowledged with reluctance. 'Wish me luck.'

Mrs Harvey shook her head, smiling her rebuke. 'You won't need it, Miss Sutton is a very graciously polite young woman.'

Maybe she was normally, but the circumstances of Chelsea being here, and the publicity attached to it were a little unusual to say the least. If the roles had been reversed Chelsea knew she wouldn't have been disposed to be polite to the other woman!

She could hear the murmur of voices in the lounge as she paused outside the door, clearing her throat noisily to let them know of her impending presence; just because Lucas didn't look like the demonstrative type didn't mean he wasn't.

The look of irritation he shot her way clearly stated he understood her ploy—and that he didn't like it one little bit. With a rueful shrug she turned towards his guest. She didn't know what she had been expecting, but there was only one word to describe Jennifer Sutton, and that was sexy.

From the top of her shiny red hair to the tips of her dainty feet Jennifer Sutton oozed sensuality! Small and delicate in the clinging black dress that was strapless as well as almost backless Jennifer Sutton must be a weapon in herself when she was in court—surely no man could resist her! She also made Chelsea feel big and clumsy—and over-dressed.

As Chelsea continued to look at the older

woman she took in the perfection of her make-up, dark shadow over sparkling green eyes, long dark mascaraed lashes, a pert nose, and wide smiling mouth painted the same colour as her shining nail-gloss. Chelsea disliked her on sight.

And the feeling appeared to be mutual as green eyes narrowed on her in critical assessment, the sharp intelligence in those green eyes at variance with the otherwise kittenish appearance. Intelligence as well as this beautiful sexuality, surely Lucas couldn't do better!

'Miss Sutton,' she greeted abruptly, wishing she could find something to criticise about the woman besides the fact that she just didn't like her, but there was nothing to criticise, everything about Jennifer Sutton was perfection. With any luck she would have a Minnie Mouse voice!

'Miss Stevens.' No such luck! Her voice was low and husky, as sultrily sexy as the rest of her.

It just wasn't fair! No one woman had the right to be so damned perfect. How could Lucas resist the other woman—Why did she *want* him to?

She had been aware all day of a feeling of anticipation in regard to seeing Lucas again, had been excited at the thought. And her jealousy now over his long-time mistress gave her an uneasy feeling. She was here to get over the heartache of losing her mother, not to give herself another heartache by falling in love with a totally unsuitable man. And she was becoming increasingly attracted to Lucas, was aware of his gaze upon her even now. He was probably comparing her to Jennifer and finding her wanting!

'I'm sure it can be Jennifer and Chelsea,' he put in smoothly. 'It's going to be very tedious listening to the two of you saying Miss Sutton and Miss Stevens all evening!'

'Of course, darling,' Jennifer smiled at him, even her teeth very straight and gleamingly white. 'I hear you're a fashion-designer, Chelsea?' she added in a bored voice.

'Training to be,' she corrected. 'I believe you're in law,' she added disinterestedly.

'One isn't *in* law, Chelsea,' the other woman told her with condescension. 'It's something that you believe in and try to uphold.'

Chelsea remained unmoved by the other woman's attitude. 'How interesting,' her tone implied the opposite. 'I'm sure you look very attractive in your court-room garb.'

Anger flashed briefly in the green eyes before it was quickly controlled. 'One doesn't enter a profession to look attractive!' Her voice had lost its silky flow now.

So the woman did have a fault after all, she took herself and life too seriously, her profession especially. Although perhaps to Lucas that was an asset not a fault; he obviously felt the same way.

'Would you care for a drink, Chelsea?' Once again Lucas cut in on the conversation, his expression warning as he looked at her.

Well she hadn't started this, for goodness' sake! Couldn't Lucas tell that his girlfriend wasn't being all that polite and friendly either? Ah well, they said love was blind, and perhaps it was.

'Am I allowed?' she mocked him.

His mouth tightened. 'I believe a small sherry would be suitable,' he bit out.

She flushed as he returned her sarcasm. 'I'd prefer a glass of wine,' she said abruptly.

'Very well.' He gave an arrogant inclination of

his head, going over to the drinks cabinet, leaving the two women alone while he did so.

'Your mother's death must have been a shock for you?'

Chelsea turned sharply at the question. 'Yes,' she answered the other woman abruptly.

Jennifer indicated with a sweep of her hand that they should sit down, positioning herself gracefully in the armchair opposite Chelsea. 'Lucas seems uncertain of how long you intend staying here?'

Her mouth tightened. 'I don't think we've actually discussed it.'

The green eyes narrowed. 'Of course I understand why your father sent you here, but you must realise that it isn't exactly—convenient for an eligible bachelor like Lucas to have a young girl staying with him indefinitely.'

Chelsea met the other woman's gaze steadily, realising that while Lucas was out of earshot the gloves of politeness were off. 'It isn't?' she returned softly, suggestively, angered into a retaliation.

'Of course not. After all——'

'Your drink,' Lucas cut across the conversation, sitting beside Chelsea as she sat on the sofa.

Jennifer Sutton looked far from pleased at the arrangement. 'Is dinner almost ready? I'm hungry,' she said waspishly. 'I missed lunch, if you remember, darling?' she added purringly.

Chelsea wondered why the two of them had missed lunch, as she knew she was supposed to do. But she couldn't help herself, the idea of Lucas possibly being so overwhelmed with passion for this kittenish woman that he had rushed her off to bed at lunchtime disgusted her.

'Hanson is your client,' Lucas shrugged. 'I

only agreed to see him because you were unavailable; it was only right that we should get together to discuss that meeting.'

Jennifer looked even less pleased as Lucas revealed the reason they had both missed lunch. 'That's what partners are for,' she snapped.

'You aren't a partner yet.'

'Lucas!' She looked shocked.

'It's only a matter of time, you know that,' he dismissed as if bored by the subject.

'And Peter's approval,' Jennifer reminded harshly. 'I don't know why he's being so difficult, I——'

'I'm sure we must be boring Chelsea with this conversation,' Lucas pointedly reminded her they weren't alone.

Chelsea looked at them with widely innocent eyes. 'On the contrary, I find it fascinating.'

Lucas's mouth tightened as he saw the mockery behind her interest. 'Fascinating or not,' he snapped, 'I'm sure dinner must be ready by now.'

For all the other woman was supposed to be so hungry she ate very sparingly of the delicious food set before them, although she monopolised most of the conversation, and Lucas along with it. But that was all right with Chelsea, she had already decided she had nothing in common with the other woman.

She offered to go and prepare the coffee after the meal as Mrs Harvey had already left for the evening, relieved to have the time away from the assertive comments of the other woman.

'You're very quiet—Careful!' Lucas moved quickly to catch the cup she had dropped at his unexpected appearance in the kitchen. 'Nervous too.' He set the cup down safely on the tray with the others, looking at her closely. 'Has this evening been too much for you?'

She stiffened warily. 'What do you mean?'

'You can hardly feel like socialising, and Jennifer isn't the most restful of people.'

'On the contrary,' Chelsea drawled. 'I find her very restful.'

His mouth twisted. 'Yes, I noticed you almost fell asleep during dessert.'

She looked up at him with guilt-stricken eyes, dismayed to realise that the boredom with the other woman's conversation that had indeed made her feel sleepy as she ate the rich sherry trifle had been noticed by this man. She hadn't realised he was even looking at her. But there was no admonishment in his eyes, only reluctant humour, a repressed devilment, almost as if they shared a joke.

'Do you think Jennifer noticed?' she grimaced.

'Do you?' he derided.

They both knew Jennifer had been so engrossed with her own conversation that she wouldn't have cared if she had noticed. 'Oh, Lucas,' Chelsea smiled her relief. 'I was so afraid just now that you were going to be angry about it.'

He frowned. 'Would that have bothered you?'

She looked at him with revealing eyes. 'You know it would,' she said huskily.

A nerve pulsed in his cheek. 'Chelsea——'

'What's keeping you two?' Jennifer burst into the kitchen, looking at them both challengingly as they stood so close together, Lucas's dark evening jacket brushing against Chelsea's dress. Jennifer arched auburn brows questioningly. 'I thought you only came to check on Chelsea, darling?' she challenged Lucas.

He straightened, crossing the room to her side. 'I did,' he acknowledged blandly. 'And I have. As you can see, she's managing just fine.'

Fury flared briefly in deep green eyes. 'More than fine, I would have said,' she snapped.

'Sorry?' Chelsea queried softly.

'You appear to have recovered very well from the grief of your mother's death,' the other woman scorned.

Chelsea paled at the accusation. 'Life has to continue,' she said dully.

'So it does,' the other woman bit out, a fierce determination in her tightly set mouth.

'Let's go back into the lounge, Jennifer,' Lucas suggested in an impatient voice. 'The coffee is almost ready.'

'Coffee?' she echoed softly, her gaze on Chelsea. 'Ah yes, the coffee,' she scorned.

Chelsea felt the constricted breath leave her body once the other couple had left the kitchen. If she had thought she had imagined that momentary flare of awareness between Lucas and herself then she was convinced it had happened by Jennifer's bitchiness when she burst in on them in that way.

What did it mean? She had been aware that her attraction towards Lucas was returning, but how did he feel about her? If he did feel attracted to her she felt sure it wasn't something he wanted to encourage. And it was something Jennifer Sutton certainly didn't want encouraged!

The other couple were sitting close together on the sofa when she came in with the tray of coffee, Jennifer's hand resting intimately against Lucas's chest as she talked up at him animatedly. They made a striking couple, Lucas so big and dark, Jennifer so petite and delicate.

An as yet unacknowledged emotion twisted in Chelsea's chest as she looked at them together, a shutter coming down over her emotions as Jennifer turned to her with triumphant eyes.

Feeling a decidedly unwanted third as she did it would have been the easiest thing in the world for her to have made her excuses and taken her own cup of coffee to her bedroom with her. But a perverse sense of not wanting to give the other woman that satisfaction made her sit in the lounge with them for another half an hour, giving no indication that she intended going to bed just yet.

Lucas seemed quite at ease with the arrangement, although Jennifer's conversation became more and more brittle as Chelsea continued to sit there, a half smile on her lips. Finally she knew she would have to leave them alone, and the thought of them being in each other's arms when she did so made her frown. She didn't like the idea of Lucas kissing that scarlet-painted mouth, possibly making love to the other woman.

'It's been a long day,' she stood up abruptly. 'I think I'll go to bed.'

'What a good idea,' Jennifer purred her satisfaction. 'I mean, you must be tired,' she added with feigned innocence.

Chelsea's mouth twisted. 'Yes, I am. It's been nice meeting you, Jennifer,' she said with the same insincerity the other woman had used when speaking to her all evening.

'I'm sure we'll meet again,' Jennifer told her confidently.

'Yes,' she answered without enthusiasm. 'Good night, Lucas.' She looked at him with suddenly shy eyes.

His smile lacked the warmth it had when they

FREE

4 BOOKS AND A SURPRISE GIFT

Here's a sweetheart of an offer that will put a smile on your lips...and 4 free Harlequin romances in your hands. Plus you'll get a secret gift, as well.

As a subscriber, you'll receive 6 new books to preview every month. Always before they're available in stores. Always for less than the retail price. Always with the right to return the shipment and owe nothing.

YES

Please send me 4 **free** Harlequin Presents novels and my **free** surprise gift. Then send me 6 new Harlequin Presents each month. Bill me for only $1.95 each (for a total of $11.70 per shipment — a savings of $1.80 off the retail price) with no extra charges for shipping and handling. I can return a shipment and cancel anytime. The 4 free books and surprise gift are mine to keep!

306 C1P UDHD

NAME_____

ADDRESS_____APT._____

CITY_____

PROV._____POSTAL CODE_____

Offer limited to one per household and not valid for present subscribers.
Prices subject to change.

AS A HARLEQUIN SUBSCRIBER, YOU'LL RECEIVE FREE...

- our monthly newsletter **Heart To Heart**
- our magazine **Romance Digest**
- special-edition **Harlequin Bestsellers** to preview for ten days without obligation

So kiss and tell us you'll give your heart to Harlequin.

FREE

4 BOOKS AND A SURPRISE GIFT

Here's a sweetheart of an offer that will put a smile on your lips...and 4 free Harlequin romances in your hands. Plus you'll get a secret gift, as well.

As a subscriber, you'll receive 6 new books to preview every month. Always before they're available in stores. Always for less than the retail price. Always with the right to return the shipment and owe nothing.

YES

Please send me 4 **free** Harlequin Presents novels and my **free** surprise gift. Then send me 6 new Harlequin Presents each month. Bill me for only $1.95 each (for a total of $11.70 per shipment — a savings of $1.80 off the retail price) with no extra charges for shipping and handling. I can return a shipment and cancel anytime. The 4 free books and surprise gift are mine to keep!

306 C1P UDHD

NAME_____

ADDRESS_____APT._____

CITY_____

PROV._____POSTAL CODE_____

Offer limited to one per household and not valid for present subscribers. Prices subject to change.

AS A HARLEQUIN SUBSCRIBER, YOU'LL RECEIVE FREE...

- our monthly newsletter **Heart To Heart**
- our magazine **Romance Digest**
- special-edition **Harlequin Bestsellers** to preview for ten days without obligation

So kiss and tell us you'll give your heart to Harlequin.

---

were in the kitchen together earlier. 'Good night, Chelsea.'

'I—er—I'll see you in the morning.' Still she lingered, wanting something more from him, and yet not knowing quite what.

'Yes,' he nodded abruptly, watching her warily.

It was that wariness, and Jennifer Sutton's gloating expression at finally being alone with Lucas, that compelled her into her next reckless action. She moved across the room, bent slightly, and kissed Lucas lingeringly on one firm cheek!

She didn't know who looked more stunned, Lucas or Jennifer! And she didn't wait around to find out, going to her bedroom without a backward glance, sure that she had left mayhem behind her.

Once in the privacy of her bedroom the defiance left her, her shoulders drooping dejectedly. All she had succeeded in doing just now had been to anger Lucas unnecessarily, and after they had once again reached a very uneasy friendship too. But she would be lying if she denied liking the feel of Lucas's firm flesh beneath her lips, and she could still taste the elusiveness of his spicy aftershave. She wondered how he had felt about the kiss. No doubt she would find out tomorrow, quite volubly if she knew him at all.

She stood under the shower for over ten minutes, just letting the hot spray wash over her, trying not to think of Lucas and Jennifer together in the lounge. If they still were in the lounge. The thought of them perhaps being across the hall in Lucas's bedroom made her groan with her own frustrated longings. She wanted Lucas herself, now realised that her own irrational behaviour this evening had been caused by jealousy of the other woman.

She donned the peach nightgown tonight, a transparent négligé in the same silky material thrown casually over a chair, the peach colour adding warmth to her skin.

It was as she was sitting in front of the dressing-table brushing her hair that she became aware of the raised voices, Lucas's sternly forceful, Jennifer's becoming increasingly shrill. They were still in the lounge, and they were arguing. Chelsea couldn't resist the temptation to open her door slightly to see what they were arguing about, and once she realised she listened unashamedly to their conversation.

'—so damned prudish,' Jennifer was accusing hotly.

'I am not being in the least prudish,' Lucas returned icily. 'I just don't think it's a good idea right now.'

'But you've stayed at my home dozens of times,' Jennifer protested.

'I'm well aware of that,' he answered calmly.

'Then why can't I stay here with you for a change?' she demanded waspishly.

So Lucas had been telling the truth when he denied having his women stay here. Obviously Jennifer felt it was time that situation changed!

'I have a guest——'

'Ah, now we're getting to the real reason for your reluctance,' Jennifer pounced. 'But Chelsea is a big girl now, and I'm sure she must be aware that we're—intimate friends.'

'I've never denied that fact,' Lucas grated. 'But neither do I intend flaunting the relationship by having you stay here tonight.'

Stunned silence greeted this statement. 'Are

you ashamed of our affair, Lucas?' Jennifer demanded softly.

'Of course not——'

'Or is it just that you don't want Chelsea to know about it?'

'She already knows we're lovers——'

'I meant tonight. You've hardly touched me tonight,' she said slowly. 'And you cancelled our last two dates. Do you still want me, Lucas?'

'You're being ridiculous now,' he rasped. 'Of course I still want you, I just think you could have chosen a better night to want to stay here.'

'Because she's here!'

'Because of Chelsea's presence in my home, yes,' he confirmed hardly.

'So you want me to leave?'

He sighed. 'You're being unreasonable, Jennifer, becoming hysterical as you did the other night.'

'How am I supposed to act, when I know that as soon as I've left you will in all probability go to that young girl's bedroom and finish what she started!'

Chelsea gasped at the accusation, and she could feel Lucas's anger emanating from here. The kiss had been a provocation, but it certainly hadn't been an invitation—had it?

'What did you say?' Lucas's voice was dangerously soft.

'Oh, don't act the innocent with me, Lucas,' Jennifer spat the words at him. 'The two of you have been looking at each other all evening——'

'That's a damned lie!'

'Is it?' she scorned. 'I don't think so. But I do think that perhaps that newspaper story wasn't so far wrong after all.'

'Would it surprise you to learn that I don't give

a damn what you think!' Lucas rasped. 'I'm at last beginning to see what it is about you that makes Peter uneasy,' he continued mercilessly. 'Professionally I've always thought you very competent, but tonight you've shown how you can over-react——'

'Over-react?' Jennifer echoed shrilly. 'I suppose I imagined interrupting something between you and Chelsea in the kitchen tonight? That I imagined that kiss?'

'There was nothing to interrupt earlier between Chelsea and me,' Lucas's voice was steely. 'And that kiss was nothing. I've been like an uncle to her since she was a child.'

'But she's a woman now!'

'It makes no difference to our relationship,' he told her arrogantly.

'If you believe that then you're a fool,' Jennifer scorned.

'I think it's time you left,' Lucas bit out. 'In fact, I think it's past time.'

'Don't worry,' she snapped. 'I'm going. And you're wrong about your precious partner Peter, I don't make him uneasy for that reason at all. He just wishes it were his bed I shared!'

'Peter is engaged to be married,' Lucas told her harshly.

'So?'

'So maybe it *should* have been his bed you shared if what you say is true,' Lucas said contemptuously. 'Because sharing mine certainly won't advance your career.'

'Why you——'

'Yes?' he prompted dangerously.

'I'm leaving!' Jennifer told him indignantly.

'I wish you would,' he snapped.

'And don't think that I'm fooled for one

minute by this argument you've provoked between us; I know damn well you're finishing things because of that little bitch!'

'Would you just leave, Jennifer.'

'With pleasure!' The apartment door could be heard slamming seconds later.

Chelsea let her breath out raggedly. God, what had she done now? Had that one little provoking kiss on Lucas's cheek caused all that? Well, if he was going to be furiously angry with her she may as well get it over with now than lay awake worrying about it. Besides, he hadn't come to bed yet, she would have heard him if he had.

He was unaware of her presence as she watched him from the lounge doorway, his back to her as he poured himself a drink, the black dinner jacket removed, the white silk shirt taut across his back.

His expression was resigned when he turned and saw her. 'Want one?' He held up his drink.

'No, thanks,' she shook her head, not moving, looking delicately ethereal in the shimmering peach gown and matching négligé.

He sat down on the sofa, stretching his long legs out in front of him. 'I suppose you heard?'

A blush coloured her cheeks as she chewed on her bottom lip. 'I——'

'It's all right, Chelsea,' he sighed, sipping his drink. 'We were talking loudly enough for the whole building to hear!'

She moved gracefully across the room. 'I just wanted to apologise.'

His eyes narrowed on her in the dimmed lighting of the room. 'For what?'

'For causing that argument between you and Jennifer, I hope you'll be able to patch things up.'

'I don't,' he stated bluntly, his expression grim. 'It's over between us.'

Her eyes widened at how cold he sounded. 'But I thought you were going to marry her?'

'Good God, no,' he said disgustedly.

'So after months together it's over between you, just like that?' she said disbelievingly.

'No, not just like that,' he rasped, 'But you heard Jennifer.'

'The whole thing was my fault,' she sighed.

Lucas shook his head. 'You can't be responsible for Jennifer's vivid imagination.'

She swallowed hard, moistening suddenly dry lips. 'She wasn't imagining anything. At least, not as far as I'm concerned she wasn't; I would like to finish what I started.' Her expression was anxious as she watched his reaction to her admission. She was laying her budding emotions towards him at his feet; she hoped he didn't trample all over them.

He had become very still, his head slowly raised to look at her. 'Chelsea——'

He was going to be patronising, she could tell. 'I'm sorry,' she dismissed jerkily. 'I didn't mean to embarrass you,' her smile was brightly meaningless. 'I'll go back to my bedroom now.'

'Chelsea!' Lucas had quickly crossed the room to grasp her arm and swing her round to face him.

'Yes?' her voice was breathless as he seemed stunned into silence. 'Lucas, what is it?' Her dark blue eyes avidly searched the taut tension of his face.

'There can't be anything between us,' he told her softly, almost absently.

'Why not?'

He moved his shoulders feelingly. 'Because whatever you're feeling right now is just a reaction to the recent shock you received, it isn't real.'

'It feels real,' she assured him huskily.

'It's just a reaction . . .'

'Is it?'

'Dear God, I don't know any more,' he groaned raggedly, his hands painful on her arms as he held her in front of him. 'Chelsea, this is wrong.'

'No.' She shook her head, her breath coming in shallow gasps.

'Kiss me again,' he ordered roughly. 'Here this time!' He dragged one of her hands up to his mouth, running her fingertips over his lips, his tongue moving to caress the sensitive tips.

She stood on tiptoe to replace her fingertips with her mouth, her lips parted to meet his, no gentleness attached to the kiss, as if they had both wanted it for too long. Lucas's mouth moved savagely against hers, as if he were driven into doing something that was beyond his control, his arms about her waist moulding her body to his.

Then he wrenched away from her, as if fighting an emotion that was a stranger to him. 'Chelsea——'

'Lucas!' she groaned her own arousal, not wanting him to fight anything, finding the passion and desire in his arms that she had always wanted, always needed. 'Please, Lucas,' she encouraged heatedly, her emotions all in her candid blue eyes as she looked up at him beseechingly.

Something akin to pain flickered in his eyes before his mouth descended to hers once more, gentler this time, sipping from her mouth, his hands moving strongly across her body, one hand lingering beneath the gentle swell of her breast as his mouth wreaked destruction with the sensitive cord in her throat, moving moistly across her shoulder, pushing the silky négligé down her arms to fall to the ground.

'I have to see all of you again,' he rasped as he slid the ribbon shoulder straps of her nightgown down her arms. 'See if I didn't just dream you after all.'

Chelsea stood proudly before him in the golden glow of the room as Lucas's lips followed the progress of the gown down her body, the proud thrust of her breasts, the nipples wetly erect after Lucas's administrations, the soft mound of her womanhood, the gentle curve of her thighs. No man had ever touched her so intimately, so completely, her body on fire with need. She clutched his shoulders with tense hands as desire peaked, quivering with the need for fulfilment.

And then his mouth was returning to hers, her head bent back as she more than met the heat of that kiss, gasping as one roughened thumb-tip moved across the tip of her breasts, feeling the heat of desire right down to her thighs.

'Lucas, make love to me!' she begged as her hands moved to the fastening of his dark trousers, feeling the throbbing heat of his own arousal against the taut material.

He sucked in a gasping breath as she touched him, suddenly thrusting her away from him, picking up her nightgown to thrust it into her resisting hands. 'This has to stop now, damn it!' His eyes glittered angrily.

Chelsea was stunned, had believed him to be as aroused as she was seconds earlier. 'Why?' she demanded to know in a strangulated voice.

'You know why!' His hands shook slightly as he helped her put on the nightgown. 'It should never have started!'

'But I want you!' Her emotions went beyond pride.

Lucas's mouth tightened even more at the admission. 'Go to your bedroom.'

'*What?*' She couldn't believe he had spoken to her in that authoritarian voice after what they had just shared!

'I said go to your room!' he ordered through clenched teeth.

Chelsea went.

CHAPTER SIX

HER pillow was very damp from all the tears she had cried after throwing herself down on the length of the bed. Lucas had dismissed her as if she were a child, and after making such beautiful love to her! She cried as much with the humiliation of that as with his rejection of her.

She had been so wrong about his coldness, Lucas could become lost in passion too, could lose all control, a deep fire in the dark warmth of his eyes. She knew that no matter how he rejected her now she could never go back to thinking of him as coldly remote, knew that beneath the façade was a man who could be controlled by passion, a man who was the way that he was simply because he wanted to hide that fierce and yet gentle passion that ruled him.

'Chelsea . . .?'

She turned sharply at the sound of his voice, quickly wiping at her tear-stained cheeks, sitting up to look at him challengingly. 'Yes?' she prompted tightly.

There was a weariness to his mouth and eyes. 'You forgot this.' He put her négligé down on the bedroom chair, moving across the room to sit on the side of her bed, gently smoothing back her hair. 'I'm sorry,' he sighed.

She swallowed hard, feeling her own instantaneous desire return at his merest touch. 'For starting it or stopping it?' she queried huskily.

He shrugged broad shoulders. 'Just sorry it happened.'

'Why?'

Heat flared in his eyes before it was quickly dampened. 'The reasons are too numerous to mention,' he shook his head.

'Try,' she encouraged throatily, determined to make him understand that nothing stood between them but his own stubbornness not to let his emotions rule his body—and hers.

'Your father sent you here for protection——'

'He sent me here because he knew I'd be safe with you,' she corrected.

'It's the same thing,' Lucas rasped.

'No,' she shook her head. 'Because I am safe with you.'

'I almost made love to you!'

'It was my decision,' she insisted calmly. 'You didn't force me into it. Jace didn't want you to protect me from emotion, just from the attention of the media.'

'Your emotions are all confused at the moment, you don't really know what you want,' Lucas told her grimly.

'I want you,' she said softly.

His jaw became rigid with disapproval. 'I'm too damned old for you.'

'You're perfect.' She touched the hardness of one cheek with loving fingers.

'You're too young for me!'

She shrugged. 'I'll get older.'

'Not soon enough for me!' Lucas stood up forcefully, moving a safe distance away from her seduction. 'No matter how much older you get there will always be fifteen years standing between us.'

Chelsea watched him with puzzled eyes. 'So when I'm thirty you'll be forty-five,' she dismissed. 'What difference does that make?'

'There's eleven more years to go before you reach thirty!' he grated derisively.

'Think of the fun we could have together in those years,' she encouraged throatily.

'You're infatuated——'

'I'm not,' she calmly shook her head. 'This is real for me, Lucas, no matter what you think. You could send me away until I'm older, but I'd still want you then, so why waste all that time?'

He drew in a ragged breath at her logic. 'You've only been here for two days——'

'So?'

'So it isn't long enough to be sure of anything, certainly not that you want to make love with someone!'

'I'm sure,' she told him softly.

'Just what is it you think you're so sure of?' he rasped.

She hesitated only momentarily. 'I love you.' She met his gaze steadily, sure beyond belief at that moment, knowing that she had fallen in love with him almost from the moment she had seen him again.

'No!'

'Yes,' she insisted firmly.

'Your mother's death——'

'Has nothing to do with the way I feel about you,' she shook her head. 'I loved my mother, but I'm not looking for a substitute parent figure. I do love you, Lucas.'

'You have no conception of the emotion,' he dismissed with deliberate callousness.

'I know I wanted to physically push Jennifer away from you tonight,' her eyes flashed with remembered anger. 'That I felt ill every time she touched you, that the thought of you making love to her, or any other woman but me, makes me feel physically sick!'

'Chelsea . . .!'

'It's true, Lucas.'

His mouth twisted. 'Has no one ever told you to keep such emotions to yourself, that unless encouraged you could embarrass someone with your intense honesty?'

'You aren't embarrassed, Lucas,' she said with confidence. 'Running scared, maybe, but——'

'Running scared!' he echoed thunderously. 'You don't know what you're talking about.'

'Don't I?' There was a half smile of satisfaction on her lips, his anger a much more honest emotion than the coldness with which he had tried to dismiss what had happened between them earlier. 'You're the one that's frightened of emotion, not me,' she shook her head.

'I am not frightened of emotion.' Suddenly he was the one to be on the defensive.

'Then why have you remained single all these years; I'm sure there must have been hundreds of women all too willing to marry you.'

'I don't intend marrying just for the sake of it,' he rasped. 'I want a wife who loves me, who wants children with me——' he broke off, seeming stunned that he had made such an admission, let alone actually meant it.

'Then why do you date women like Jennifer Sutton? Oh I'll admit she wouldn't hesitate to marry you, but she's also obviously a career-woman. And she would never dream of ruining that wonderful figure while she had your children!' Chelsea derided.

'I'm sure it can't have escaped your notice,' his mouth twisted without humour, 'but Jennifer and I won't be seeing each other socially again.'

'I realise that,' she shrugged. 'Just as I'm equally sure you will quickly replace her with someone else who is completely unsuitable.'

'To you perhaps, but not to me! God, why am I bothering to defend myself in this way?' He was impatient with himself.

'Because you know I want you, because I love you, because I would love to have children with you,' she told him with husky softness.

'This is ridiculous,' he stormed over to the door. 'You don't know what you're saying!'

'Oh, I know,' she nodded. 'Think about it, Lucas,' she encouraged throatily.

'There's nothing to think about,' he shook his head, his expression remote. 'And I'm sure that when you come to your senses you'll regret what you've just told me.'

Chelsea gave him a pitying smile. 'I'm not some hysterical virgin who thinks she has to declare undying love just because she got carried away with passion with a man,' she derided.

Lucas halted in his tracks, looking at her with narrowed eyes. 'You aren't a virgin?'

'Oh yes, I am,' she told him softly. 'And I'm glad that I am. I want you to be my first lover.'

'You're insane!' he bit out.

She smiled happily at his outraged confusion. 'I can also be very determined when I want something.'

'Me?'

'Yes,' she confirmed lightly.

He shook his head dazedly. 'I've never met anyone like you before.'

'That's what I'm hoping,' she nodded.

His eyes narrowed. 'You're really serious about this?'

'So serious I think we should try to have our

first baby by next Christmas. I think Christmas would be a nice time to have a baby, don't you. Think of the lovely names we could—Lucas?' she queried mockingly as he stormed out of the room, falling back on the pillows with a dreamy smile on her face.

Lucas's son, with his warm brown eyes and dark hair. And maybe a daughter later on for her. All she had to do was convince Lucas that he could love her as she loved him. She knew it was possible, but she also knew that Lucas's will was far stronger than her own, that for the majority of the time he could control and manipulate his emotions. But tonight had seen a crack in those emotions, and she intended for it to widen and widen until he couldn't stop the love pouring out.

She loved Lucas McAdams! It was incredible that until a short time ago she had been so miserable. Now she had hope, a dream for the future, a love that would help her cope with the loss of her mother, but not replace her as Lucas accused her of doing.

And she wanted Lucas physically in a way she had never dreamt of wanting Randy, the boy she had once thought to marry. Thank God, she hadn't! Because she had a feeling she would have fallen in love with Lucas whatever her married state had been.

'You've seemed happier the last few days,' Mrs Harvey smiled at her.

'I am happier,' Chelsea nodded, sitting in the kitchen eating her breakfast, as she had done for the past week, the housekeeper having thawed enough to allow that.

'I'm glad the shock of your mother's death is lessening.'

'Yes,' she sobered.

The first numbed heartache of her mother's death had indeed gone, a dull ache whenever she thought of all that beauty now gone, acceptance that it had gone, that, no matter what recriminations she gave herself, her mother was gone, and there was nothing she could do about it now except go on with her own life. And Lucas had become that life.

She thought with amusement of the last three days, of his deliberate avoidance of spending time alone with her, almost as if he suspected she might pounce on him if they were. Consequently he was gone in the mornings before she got up, did not come home for lunch, and worked late every evening, disappearing into his study with his dinner on a tray when he did get home. It was that very avoidance of her that gave her hope he might come to care for her; why else would he need so desperately to stay away from her?

Yes, she was happy, in a quietly confident way. She hadn't come to England looking for love; it had been the last thing on her mind when she left Los Angeles. And she knew that Lucas wasn't the ideal man for her to have fallen in love with, she just couldn't help herself.

Mrs Harvey's mouth firmed as the telephone rang. 'If it's one of those reporters again!' she warned ominously. 'I don't know how they got hold of this number.'

Chelsea watched anxiously as the other woman took the call; several really persistent reporters had rung the apartment the last few days, much to Lucas's anger. A few tersely cold calls to the owners of the newspapers had put a stop to most of them, but one man kept persisting. John Anderson. After the way he had deceived her she would have thought he would have the decency to just leave her alone, but he telephoned several times a day wanting to talk to her. She always refused.

'Yes, Mr Stevens,' Mrs Harvey beamed at Chelsea as the caller identified himself as her father. 'She's right here.' She held out the receiver to the waiting Chelsea, quietly returning to the kitchen once Chelsea had taken it.

'Jace,' she greeted with relief. 'Where have you been?' she demanded to know. 'I've been expecting to hear from you for days.'

'I know, Princess,' he sighed, sounding very, very tired. 'I'm sorry I haven't called before.'

'Are you all right?' she asked with concern; he didn't sound it.'

'I'm fine.'

She didn't believe that for a moment! 'Where are you?'

'I'm—Just at a friend's, Princess,' he dismissed. 'I shall be going back to Los Angeles soon anyway; I have to face it some time.'

'Are you sure you're all right?' she persisted. 'You sound sort of—strange.'

'Thanks!'

'You know what I mean,' she said impatiently.

'It must be a bad line,' he dismissed again. 'Because I feel fine. I just wanted to know what you've been up to?'

She tensed. 'Me?' Oh God, he had found out about the newspaper article after all!

'I just spoke to Lucas, and he seemed decidedly odd when I asked how you were.'

'Odd?' she delayed.

'Reluctant,' her father amended. 'What have you done to the poor guy, Princess?'

He *didn't* know about the newspaper article!

'I'm not sure you're ready for this,' she said slowly.

'Princess?' his voice sharpened with concern.

'I've fallen in love with him,' she admitted ruefully.

'And Lucas?'

'You don't sound surprised, or——or disapproving?' she frowned at his calm reaction.

'Why should I disapprove of Lucas, he's a good man.'

'A very good man,' she agreed. 'So good he says he's too old for me.'

'You'll grow up.'

'Exactly what I said,' she laughed happily. 'Oh, Jace, I wish he could hear you.'

'He sounds harassed enough already. Are you really sure about this, Princess?'

'Positive,' she said without hesitation.

'I thought you were equally as positive about Randy once upon a time,' he reminded dryly.

'Not like with Lucas,' she dismissed. 'I loved Randy as a friend, and thought it was the sort of love that led to marriage. With Lucas I don't care if it leads to marriage or not, I just want to be with him.'

'I understand, Princess,' Jace sighed. 'I guess my little girl has finally grown up.'

'Lucas isn't convinced,' she told him regretfully.

'I'm sure you'll find a way to convince him,' her father said dryly. 'I bet he's never run into anyone as completely forthright as you before.'

'He does seem a little surprised,' she mused, sobering suddenly. 'But are you sure you're all right,' she still persisted. 'I could come home if——'

'No! Er—no, I don't think so, Princess,' his

voice was less harsh the second time he spoke. 'Give it at least another week or so.'

'But if I can help you——'

'The best way to help me is to stay where you are,' he said dully. 'This is something I have to sort out alone. Besides,' he added teasingly, 'you don't want to leave Lucas to the charms of some other woman, do you?'

'No . . .' she acknowledged slowly, thinking of Jennifer Sutton. Lucas worked with the other woman every day, and although he had been adamant that things were over between them after the vicious scene she had overhead, she had no doubt Jennifer could make herself very appealing if she wanted to. And for an ambitious woman like that Lucas was a good catch.

'Don't worry about things back here,' Jace told her lightly. 'I can handle it. You sound as if you have your hands full trying to convince Lucas you're serious.'

'He can be very stubborn,' she conceded.

Jace laughed softly. 'That has to be the understatement of the year! But give him time, you haven't been there very long. He doesn't know yet how stubborn *you* can be.'

She wasn't completely convinced by her father's jovial mood, sure that her first instincts had been right, that the strain of the publicity attached to her mother's death was proving too much for him to handle alone. She felt she should go back to be with him.

'He wants you to stay here,' Lucas told her when she made the suggestion to him over lunch, one of the rare times he had come home for it.

'But I could help him,' she protested.

'Have you forgotten, he still thinks you believe your mother's death to be from natural causes?'

'And you said he would have to realise one day that I know the truth, so why not now?'

Lucas sighed, looking strained himself, lines of tiredness beside his eyes. 'I don't think he could handle it just now.'

'And I don't think *you* can handle me staying,' she told him ruefully.

He stiffened, his mouth tight. 'What's that supposed to mean?' he snapped.

She leant her elbows on the table, her chin in her hands. 'It hasn't escaped my notice that you've been avoiding me.'

'Rubbish!'

'Ever since the other night,' she finished pointedly, watching him closely.

He gave a deep sigh, unconsciously crumbling the uneaten roll on his plate between steely fingers. 'I think it's best if we forget the other night,' he bit out tautly.

Chelsea shook her head. 'I can't. Can you?'

'I'm trying,' he grated grimly.

'Jace thinks the two of us loving each other is a wonderful idea,' she told him with calm innocence, waiting for the explosion. She didn't have to wait long!

'*What?*' he thundered.

Her mouth quirked into a smile at his outrage, pleased to have elicited a response from him other than the cold politeness he had shown her on the rare occasions they had met the last few days. 'I told Jace about us, and he——'

'There is no *us* to tell him about, damn it!' Lucas threw down his napkin on the table before standing up to glare down at her with blazing brown eyes. 'I'm sure he was shocked out of his mind to think I'd been making love to a teenager!'

She was aware of the reluctant question behind his words. 'I didn't tell him about that——'

'Thank God for that!'

'But I did tell him how I feel about you. He likes the idea,' she shrugged.

'What idea?' Lucas demanded impatiently.

'The two of us getting married.'

His eyes widened in shock before closing again in disbelief. 'I can't believe you told your father that,' he shook his head.

'Why can't you?' she frowned.

'Because—well, because—Because it isn't true, that's why,' he said in exasperation. 'Chelsea, tell me you didn't tell Jace such a thing.'

'I could tell you that,' she agreed slowly.

'Thank God!'

'But it wouldn't be the truth,' she added ruefully.

'You did tell him?' Lucas rasped.

'Yes,' she nodded.

'Chelsea!' Lucas breathed raggedly. 'How could you do such a thing? Doesn't he have enough to worry about without burdening him with this nonsense?'

'I told you, he was pleased about it,' she insisted. 'And it isn't nonsense.'

He gave an impatient glance at his wristwatch. 'I don't have the time to argue with you now, I have to be back in court in a few minutes. But this discussion is far from over,' he warned as he pulled the charcoal grey jacket on over his fitted waistcoat. 'It might seem amusing to you to have put me in this awkward position, but I can assure you I don't find it in the least funny!'

'I can see that.' She stood up to straighten the already straight collar of his jacket, using the excuse just to get close to him. 'But one day you will,' she promised him before standing on tiptoe to kiss him lingeringly on the mouth, Lucas momentarily too stunned by the unexpected caress to move away, Chelsea's arms moving about his waist as he finally would have done so.

'Mr McAdams, I—Oh!' A stunned Mrs Harvey came to a halt in the doorway, too surprised to do anything but stare at them.

Lucas pushed Chelsea viciously away from him, his expression clearly showing his displeasure. 'What is it, Mrs Harvey?' he rasped growlingly.

'I—Well, I—I wondered if you would be in to dinner this evening.' The poor woman sounded flustered, obviously disturbed by the kiss she had just witnessed between her employer and his young guest.

'Yes,' he answered Mrs Harvey, but his steely gaze was fixed on Chelsea. 'Yes, I'll be here for dinner at seven o'clock,' he added grimly.

'Very well.' The distressed woman returned to her kitchen at top speed.

Chelsea was smiling when Lucas turned back to her; she couldn't help it.

'You know why I've decided to be back early tonight?' he asked her coldly.

'So you can finally spend some time with me, I hope,' she grinned impishly.

His mouth thinned into an angry line. 'Chelsea, you are a guest in my home, I will not have you disrupting my household in this way.'

She opened innocently wide blue eyes. 'What did I do wrong now?'

He sighed his impatience. 'Don't make the mistake of believing your own publicity,' he rasped.

'Sorry?' she frowned.

'Your young friend Anderson may have implied that we're having an affair,' he reminded grimly. 'But that's no reason for you to actually believe that we are!'

'I didn't make that publicity,' she flared angrily. 'John distorted the facts to get a story!'

'He only printed what you told him,' Lucas shook his head.

'But he made it into something it wasn't,' she protested her innocence. 'Not then, anyway.'

'Aren't you doing the same thing?' Lucas reasoned. 'You're far away from home, have suffered a recent emotional trauma, you aren't seeing things in perspective at the moment.'

Chelsea shook her head, a half smile to her lips. 'You can't *talk* me out of loving you, Lucas. Okay, I accept that it's happened quickly, unexpectedly, but if I hadn't met you now I would have met you some other time, and I would still have loved you. Some things are just fated to be.'

He gave her an impatient glare. 'We'll talk about this again tonight,' he dismissed. 'In the meantime, try not to shock Mrs Harvey more than she already is.'

'I doubt that I could,' she said with amusement, sitting down to finish her coffee, looking at Lucas beneath lowered lashes. 'So far she's seen me returning your pyjama jacket to your bedroom my first day here, leaving your bedroom the morning after that in a sexy nightgown and négligé, and you following me out of the room wearing only a towel. And now she's actually seen us kissing each other.'

'Oh God!' Lucas groaned disgustedly.

'Yes,' she smiled. 'So unless she actually walks in on us making love I don't think things could get any worse.'

'I'm going back to work,' he rasped.

'I'll see you later,' she acknowledged throatily.

'I wish you would behave yourself,' he scowled.

'Do you?' she mocked, her head back in challenge.

He gave her a look that spoke volumes, before closing the door forcefully behind him as he left.

Poor Lucas, he obviously wasn't going to accept her love gracefully. From what he had told her of his childhood he had had to work for any praise and affection that he got, and now he didn't know when to accept the latter when it was freely given to him. She would just have to stay around long enough to convince him.

As with that other evening when she had known he was to be joining her for dinner she was in the lounge waiting for him, the whisky and dash of water in a glass in her hand, a smile to her lips.

Lucas took the drink and swallowed it all down without saying a word, sparing not a glance for the appearance she had taken such care over. Her hair was tightly coiled back from her face to be secured on the top of her head in a sleek knot, made to look darker in its confines, the severity of the style throwing into prominence the haunted beauty of her face, the long white dress shot through with silver clinging lovingly to her slender curves, slit almost to her thigh on one side to allow freedom of movement, showing a tantalising glimpse of bare flesh. But for all the notice Lucas took of her before he strode from the room to shower and change she could have been wearing a sack and have soot on her face and hair!

She poured him a second drink, carrying it very

carefully as she followed him to his bedroom, sitting down on the bed as she waited for him to come out of the adjoining bathroom where she could hear him taking a shower. She had to be sitting down so that he couldn't propel her straight back out of the room!

He was drying his hair as he came out of the bathroom, the customary towel draped about his hips, coming to an abrupt halt when he saw her, controlling his anger with effort. 'Wouldn't you say this was a *blatant* invasion of my privacy?' he bit out between taut lips.

'Blatant,' she acknowledged softly, able to smell the spicy tang of his aftershave, his shampoo smelling of limes. She stood up, holding out the drink to him. 'I thought you might need this.'

He shook his head. 'I don't.'

'Oh,' she put it down on the dressing-table, pressing her hands tightly together at his abrupt rebuff.

His eyes were very dark as he looked at her. 'I need something else.'

'Oh?' She hadn't missed the harsh intensity of his voice, the tension in his body.

He threw down the towel he had been drying his hair with. 'Did you style your hair like that on purpose?'

Her eyes widened. 'I didn't think you had noticed,' she said softly.

'I notice everything about you,' he told her huskily. 'From that scrap of provocation you call a gown, to the equally provocative style of your hair.'

Chelsea frowned, touching the smooth hair at her temple. 'What's wrong with it?' It had taken her over an hour to perfect!

'There's nothing wrong with it,' Lucas growled, his expression closed. 'It makes your neck and throat look so slender I could snap it with one hand, reveals the perfect beauty of your face, makes your eyes look like huge sapphires. You look beautiful, Chelsea, and yet I'm still going to release every silky strand,' he deftly began to remove each securing pin.

Chelsea's eyes were wider than ever as she stared up at him, so close now she could see the smoothness of his jaw where he had just shaved, one of those men that had a 'five o'clock' stubble. 'Why?' she moistened the sudden dryness of her lips.

'So that I can spread it across the pillow while I make love to you.' He threaded his fingers into the silkiness so that it cascaded down her back. 'No woman should be allowed to have such beautiful hair.' He looked at it in wonder. 'Are you a siren, come to lure me to my doom?'

'Oh, Lucas.' She gently smoothed the frown from his brow, angry with the people who had taught him to be wary of love, distrustful of it, as if to give it took something away from him rather than gave something back to him as it was supposed to do. 'Kiss me, darling,' she urged. 'It's been so long, and I ache for you.'

'Dear God, I can't fight you when you're like this,' he groaned raggedly, cupping her face with his hands.

'Why should you want to?' she rained fevered kisses along his jaw.

'Because this isn't real,' he insisted, shuddering in reaction to her lips at his throat and ears. 'You'll wake up one morning and realise you don't love me at all.'

She wanted to tell him he was wrong, but she

knew he wouldn't believe her, that she would
have to show him how she felt. Her lips travelled
slowly down his chest, lingering on the hard nubs
nestled among the dark hair, her tongue flicking
across the taut flesh as Lucas gasped in reaction.
She was kneeling before him as she kissed his
navel, her tongue dipping in and out of the warm
cavern, protesting at the interruption to her
lovemaking as he pulled her back up to her feet.

His gaze was searching. 'I might seem as if I'm
made of stone,' he warned hardly, 'but I'm not. If
you kiss me any more I'm going to carry you over
to that bed, strip the clothes from your body, and
possess you until you can't think straight. I
warned you before that I'm only a man, that I
can only take so much provocation.'

Chelsea's answer was to gently pull the towel
from about his hips, her gaze following the sleek
lines of his body as he sucked in his breath.
'You're beautiful,' she breathed softly, a slow
smile of wonder on her lips, his naked body
magnificent, his arousal already strong and hard.
'Please take me to bed, Lucas,' she pleaded
achingly.

His gaze didn't leave her flushed face as he
swung her up in his arms, her own arms clinging
around his neck as she snuggled against him. He
lay her gently down on the bed, poised above her
as he stared down at her with dark eyes. 'You're
like a beautiful, bright, shining star,' he muttered
gruffly. 'I don't want to tarnish that.'

'Making love to me will make me *feel*
beautiful,' she assured him, pulling him down to
her.

But before their lips could make contact the
doorbell rang, Lucas jerking away from her as if
someone had slapped him.

'Ignore it,' Chelsea urged, holding out her arms to him, letting them fall disappointedly to her side as she watched him pull on his towelling robe, tying it tightly at his waist.

'It must be someone I know to have got past security,' he said grimly.

'You can't go to the door like that,' she reminded him, getting to her feet, looking just as lovely as she had earlier, her gown uncreased, her hair looking as if it were supposed to be styled this way.

Lucas looked down ruefully at his near nakedness. 'You're right, I can't.'

'I'll go,' she offered tersely, lingering in the doorway. 'Lucas, we aren't just going to pretend tonight didn't happen too, are we?' she pleaded.

He put up a hand to his temple. 'I don't know, I have to think. But you're right, I can't keep making love to you and then expecting you to forget it happened. We'll talk as soon as we've got rid of our unwanted guest. I'll join you as soon as I'm dressed.'

From the way he said the latter Chelsea had the feeling that he too suspected who that guest was; Jennifer Sutton. And that fact alone told her that Jennifer *hadn't* given up her chase of Lucas, that as she had suspected the other woman had regretted her impassioned outburst that night.

She was frowning as she opened the door, wondering what she was going to say to Jennifer Sutton, if there were something she could say to the other woman to get her to leave before Lucas joined them.

Her mouth fell open in surprise as she opened the door and saw who stood there. 'Camilla!'

CHAPTER SEVEN

THE other woman gave a wan smile of acknowledgment, a tall leggy young woman with a shoulder-length cloud of lustrous black hair, and the most exquisitely beautiful face Chelsea had ever seen.

But her friend looked tired at this moment, a sad droop to her mouth, her shoulders hunched over dejectedly. She carried a single suitcase, her knuckles showing white as she gripped it.

'Can I come in?' she prompted huskily as Chelsea continued to stare at her.

'I—Of course.' She stepped back, her mind racing at Lucas's sister being here, and obviously intending to stay. Her own talk with Lucas was sure to be put off now, which meant Lucas would have time to build up all the same defences that had previously plagued him. She liked Camilla, was pleased to see her, but she couldn't help wishing the other woman had chosen any night but this one to arrive.

The cream coat Camilla wore owed more to fashion than warmth, and she discarded it in the warmth of the apartment, leaving her suitcase in the hallway, on her way through to the lounge, the cream dress that matched the coat styled to her slender body.

'Where's Lucas?' she asked as Chelsea remained silent. 'Has he gone out?'

'He's dressing,' she answered abruptly, colour entering her cheeks as she realised how that sounded to her own ears if not to Camilla's unsuspecting ones. 'For dinner,' she added awkwardly.

Camilla nodded abruptly, obviously seeing nothing unusual in that. 'Has he been home long?'

'Not long, no,' she answered jerkily. 'Er—I don't think he's expecting you.' There hadn't been a lot of time for conversation this evening, but she felt sure Lucas wouldn't have started making love to her if he expected his sister to arrive at any moment!

'No, he isn't,' Camilla acknowledged curtly. 'It was a sudden decision.'

'How's Jace?'

'Jace?' the other woman frowned at the question, looking more tired than ever.

Chelsea nodded. 'He mentioned that you were still helping him with things out there. I wondered if you had seen him before you left?'

'Your father is staying at a friend's villa in France,' came the abrupt reply.

'France?' she echoed dazedly. 'But that's just across the sea.'

'Yes,' Camilla nodded wearily.

'Then why doesn't he come to England?' she frowned.

'He might be recognised here,' Camilla shrugged. 'Lucas is a long time dressing,' she frowned.

Judging from his state of arousal when she had left him he needed this time to be respectable enough to present himself in front of a third person! 'I'm sure he'll join us in a moment,' she dismissed.

Camilla prowled restlessly about the room, her movements jerky and uncoordinated, which was very unusual for her.

'Is there anything wrong?' Chelsea frowned.

'No,' Camilla answered sharply. 'I just need to talk to Lucas.'

She swallowed hard. 'Jace didn't send you here, did he?' It had suddenly occurred to her that perhaps her father had had second thoughts about Lucas and herself and had asked Camilla to intervene. She had certainly arrived at an inconvenient time!

'Jace?' Camilla echoed abruptly. 'Why should he send me here?'

She sighed. 'To break up Lucas and me.'

'Lucas and you . . .?' The other woman's stunned reaction was enough to convince Chelsea she had been wrong in that respect at least; Camilla had no idea what she was talking about! 'Have the two of you been arguing?' Camilla further confirmed her ignorance of knowing anything about a romantic involvement between her brother and Chelsea.

'A little,' Chelsea replied truthfully.

'Well, Jace isn't aware of it,' Camilla dismissed in a preoccupied voice. 'So the two of you haven't been getting along, hm?' she added ruefully.

'We didn't, at first,' she acknowledged guardedly. 'But we're okay together now.'

'That's good.' Camilla lost interest in the subject, glancing impatiently towards the door.

'Are you sure there's nothing wrong?' Chelsea frowned at her friend, worried by how pale and drawn she looked, wishing Lucas would hurry up; something was obviously troubling Camilla badly, and she wasn't inclined to discuss it with Chelsea.

'Nothing,' the other woman answered in a bitter voice. 'What on earth can be keeping Lucas?' she frowned, echoing Chelsea's thoughts.

'I'll go and tell him you're here——'

'That isn't necessary,' he cut in icily, looking at his sister with narrowed, disapproving eyes. 'Camilla, what are you doing here?' he rasped.

Chelsea was taken aback by his aggression as much by his appearance, a cream shirt partly unbuttoned down his chest, black trousers moulded to his lean legs and thighs, his damp hair evidence that he had taken a second shower. Colour flooded her cheeks as she guessed the reason for that.

'Is Jace with you?' he bit out before Camilla had time to answer his first question.

She shook her head wearily. 'I'm alone.'

'And Jace?'

'Still in France.'

'Does he know you've come here?' Lucas demanded to know unrelentingly.

Camilla blushed. 'Look, Lucas, if I'm not welcome I can always go to——'

'I didn't say you weren't welcome,' he rasped harshly. 'I just want to know if you told Jace where you were going or if you just left.'

'He knows,' Camilla said flatly, looking awkwardly at Chelsea. 'I was in France with your father before coming here,' she explained uncomfortably.

That much she had gathered, what she couldn't understand was why Lucas was so angry at his sister for leaving and coming here. Hadn't she done enough for them, helped them out enough? She was only a friend, albeit a good one, and they had imposed on her long enough. Lucas was being unreasonable.

'Lucas, I'm sure Jace understood Camilla has her own life to lead,' she defended the other woman. 'She's been such a help to us, you both have.'

His eyes narrowed, his mouth firming. 'Why don't you go and check on dinner,' he suggested hardly. 'I'm sure it must be ready by now.'

She went to the kitchen with an angry set to her mouth, feeling a little like Mrs Harvey must do when dismissed in the same way. She hardly recognised this Lucas as the same one who had been making such tender love to her only minutes ago, his defences back in place much more quickly than she would have liked, knowing that the promised talk was definitely out now that Camilla was here. But that was no reason for him to be so terse with both Camilla and herself, and there was a sparkle of challenge in her eyes as she returned to the lounge.

'I'm not condemning you, Camilla,' Lucas was almost gentle now. 'I understand what you're going through, I just think that coming back here now will solve nothing.'

'But it was so awful, Lucas,' his sister choked. 'The things the newspapers are saying about us!'

'I still think you should have stayed and supported Jace,' he told her sternly. 'It was the only thing you could do in the circumstances.'

'Maybe the only thing *you* could have done in the same circumstances,' Camilla said accusingly. 'But I don't happen to be made out of the same strength of character.'

'Camilla——'

'Leave me alone, Lucas,' she snapped. 'Just tell me if I can stay here or not, because if not I——'

'Of course you can stay here,' he interrupted in a steely voice. 'Stay until you feel ready to go back.'

'I'm not sure that I'm going back.'

'Camilla!' Lucas strode after his sister as she rushed past Chelsea and into the bedroom the two women would have to share. He stopped outside the room as the door was firmly closed in his face. 'Camilla, hiding in there isn't going to change a thing,' he warned, silence greeting this comment. 'What do I tell Jace if he telephones?' he sighed.

'He won't,' came Camilla's muttered response.

Lucas's expression was grim as he returned back to the lounge, ignoring Chelsea as she would have spoken, walking straight over to the drinks cabinet and pouring himself some whisky into a glass, not even bothering to add the usual water as he swallowed it all down without pause.

'Lucas——'

'Your damned family has caused nothing but trouble almost from the moment we all met you,' he cruelly cut in on her tentative query.

'Lucas!' She was stunned by the vehemence of his attack.

He poured himself another whisky, drinking it slower this time. 'First your father and mother,' he continued grimly. 'And now you're trying to tie me up in the same knots. Well I won't have it, Chelsea,' he slammed the empty glass down on the table. 'Stay out of my way for the rest of your time here,' he grated. 'Because if you don't I'm not going to be answerable for the consequences!'

That he was threatening violence she didn't doubt, and she didn't even know what she had done to merit such anger. 'Has Camilla been caught up in the bad publicity in the States?' It was the only explanation she could think of in connection with the conversation she had been witness to. And that surely couldn't be anyone's fault but the ghoulish public.

Lucas's mouth was tight. 'I suggest you ask Camilla about that,' he bit out harshly.

She grimaced. 'I don't think she's in the mood to talk about it.'

'Then you'll just have to leave it, won't you,' he rasped with sarcasm. 'Is the dinner ready?'

She flinched at the way he just dismissed her concern over Camilla. 'Yes, it is,' she snapped, turning on her heel. 'And I hope you enjoy eating it!' She slammed into the bedroom after Camilla.

The other woman wasn't in the bedroom now, so she assumed she must be in the adjoining bathroom. What a disaster of an evening, and it had started out so promisingly too! Now all she wanted to do was sit and cry.

Camilla's expression became guarded as she came back from the bathroom and saw Chelsea sitting on one of the two single beds, wearing trousers and a thick sweater now, her beautiful face bare of make-up. 'Aren't you having dinner?' she enquired lightly.

Chelsea shook her head. 'Suddenly I don't feel hungry any more.'

The other woman's expression became even more wary. 'Oh?'

She sighed raggedly. 'Your brother has to be one of the most difficult men I know.'

'That I know too,' Camilla agreed, taking some flat shoes out of her partly unpacked suitcase before putting them on.

'You weren't supposed to say that,' Chelsea grimaced.

'Why not?' Camilla shrugged narrow shoulders. 'It's the truth, he *is* a difficult man. He's also unyielding, unreasonable, bossy, arrogant, and a bit of a tyrant. And I love him,' she pulled a face.

'So do I,' she nodded.

'Chelsea . . .?' Camilla looked startled.

'Don't worry,' she sighed. 'It isn't reciprocated. He says I'm too young for him, juvenile, in fact.'

Camilla's dark eyes so like her brother's were wide with surprise. 'Lucas knows how you feel?'

'I told him,' she nodded.'

Camilla began to smile, relaxing. 'You know, Chelsea, when I arrived I was feeling so miserable I just wanted to crawl into a corner and die. You've made me feel better already.'

She made a rueful face. 'I suppose my loving Lucas is funny——'

'No, not funny at all,' Camilla hastily assured her. 'But I'm sure Lucas's reaction to it is. I can just see the expression on my stuffy brother's face when you told him you loved him, a mixture between shock and anger.'

'You forgot the dismay,' Chelsea told her with a grimace.

'Poor Lucas,' Camilla smiled again.

Chelsea moved restlessly about the room. 'Poor me, you mean. Why is it that everyone feels sorry for Lucas, *I'm* the one who loves a man who doesn't even believe in the emotion!'

Camilla's eyes narrowed. 'You've told Jace about this?'

'Yes,' she sighed.

'What's his opinion?'

'That I have a long struggle ahead of me to convince Lucas I'm serious,' she dismissed. 'If he talks to me much more the way he did just now I'm not sure that I want to!'

Camilla touched her arm consolingly. 'Lucas is angry with me, not you.'

'But *why*?'

'It's a long story.'

'And you don't feel like telling it right now,' she realised understandingly.

'Lucas is very wrong about you, Chelsea,' Camilla touched her cheek affectionately. 'You're very adult.'

She gave a rueful smile. 'I wish I could get him to believe that.'

'Maybe you have,' Camilla shrugged. 'Did I mention the fact that Lucas is also stubborn, and very self-sufficient? He doesn't like leaving himself open to pain, Chelsea.'

'Doesn't like his emotions to be involved, you mean,' she grimaced.

'That's about it,' the other woman nodded. 'You know, hearing about your problems has taken my mind off my own,' she realised dazedly.

'Maybe if you tell me yours it will have the same effect on me,' she encouraged.

'I'll tell you, Chelsea,' she nodded gently. 'But not just yet. Okay?'

'Okay,' she agreed with a shrug.

Camilla gave her a considering look. 'You know, I'm going out for a walk, and you look good enough to eat, so why don't you rejoin Lucas for dinner?'

'Because I just more or less told him what to do with his dinner!'

Camilla laughed softly. 'Why miss one of Mrs Harvey's wonderful dinners just because you're angry with Lucas?' she reasoned.

'Because I'm afraid I may tip it over Lucas's head if he's rude to me again!'

'All the more reason,' Camilla encouraged. 'A bowl of gravy tipped all over him may do him good.'

She heaved a deep sigh. 'Lucas doesn't think that anything I do is good.'

Camilla sobered. 'Lucas isn't very adept at showing his emotions, but that doesn't mean he doesn't care. He's looked after me all his life, and yet he's never once said he loves me.'

'He does though,' Chelsea frowned.

'Exactly.'

'But he can be so cruel when he wants to be!'

'When he wants to be,' Camilla echoed. 'It isn't a wanton, hot-headed cruelty, it's something he thinks out and acts upon. He always has his reasons.'

'You know,' steel entered Chelsea's voice, 'I think I will go and have dinner with him after all. And I'll be so nice to him he'll wonder what's hit him.'

Lucas was sitting in an armchair when she entered the lounge, the newspaper held up in front of his face, his tightly gripping fingers showing he was still angry. Well so was she, and she had more reason to be!

'Dinner will be getting cold,' she told him loudly, watching with glee as he crumpled his newspaper as he jumped in surprise.

He lowered the paper slowly, his eyes steely. 'I thought you weren't eating dinner?'

She raised innocent brows. 'I didn't say that,' she shook her head, her hair still loose down to her waist.

'When you stormed out of here——'

'When I went to talk to Camilla, you mean,' she corrected. 'I told you to start dinner without me.'

His mouth twisted. 'That isn't the way it sounded!'

'Well it's the way I meant it,' she glibly lied.

'Chelsea——'

'Yes?' she looked at him with challenging eyes.

'Nothing,' he rasped, throwing down the

newspaper in an uncustomary gesture. 'As you said, dinner will be getting cold.' He followed her through to the dining-room, his mouth tight.

Chelsea was so sweet to him for the rest of the evening it was sickening. But she had the satisfaction of knowing she had disconcerted Lucas; he just didn't know what to make of her behaviour!

'How did it go?' Camilla asked sleepily as Chelsea joined her in the bedroom, having returned from her walk shortly after nine and gone straight to bed.

'He's confused,' Chelsea said with satisfaction, undressing in the darkness so that she didn't disturb the other woman too much.

'Keep him on the run, Chelsea,' Camilla advised with a tired yawn. 'He has to stop for breath some time.'

That was true, but there was no guarantee that when he did stop it would be with her. As she lay in bed unable to sleep she knew Camilla lay awake too, despite her rather obvious efforts to look tired a few minutes ago. But she respected the other woman's privacy, as Camilla respected hers, and finally she did fall asleep.

Camilla had gone from the adjoining bed when she woke the next morning, and after looking at her watch she knew that Lucas would have left for work too, taking her time about dressing, in no hurry to start being sociable when she felt so *un*sociable. She had a headache this morning, felt decidedly unlike her robust self.

She could hear voices in the lounge, frowning as she realised Lucas must be at home after all, one of the voices decidedly male. 'I thought you—John!' All tiredness left her as she realised the identity of the person Camilla was talking to, turning to glare accusingly at John before turning stricken eyes to Camilla, turning back to John as Camilla seemed innocent of his troublemaking, her smile friendly. 'What are you doing here?' she asked John flatly.

He had stood up at her entrance. 'I came to see you.' He was watching her closely.

Her body braced as if for attack; she hadn't seen him since that day he had so skilfully pumped all that information out of her that had gone into his story. 'How did you get in?' she demanded to know.

Camilla was listening to the exchange with a puzzled expression. 'I met Mr Anderson outside, and——'

'And naturally he charmed you into bringing him up here,' Chelsea finished with contempt for the man. 'I hope you've been careful what you've said to him, Camilla,' her contemptuous gaze still rested on John even though she spoke to the other woman, his expression uncomfortable, 'because it will all be in print tomorrow.'

'What!' Camilla stared at the reporter with horror in her eyes.

'John is a reporter, Camilla,' she said with distaste. 'I made the mistake last week of thinking he was just a nice man offering me a little sympathy and a shoulder to cry on, and lo and behold the next morning every word I'd told him appeared on the front page of his newspaper!'

'Not quite every word,' he reminded softly.

She flushed at the truth of that. 'Almost every word,' she conceded grudgingly.

'And I don't have a newspaper,' he corrected. 'I'm freelance.'

'I'm sure you didn't have a shortage of offers for that disgusting story you wrote last week!'

'I had only a lukewarm response to the story I originally submitted.'

'Really?' she said disinterestedly. 'So you decided to spice it up a little to really get their interest, hm?'

'I'd think I'd better leave the two of you alone to talk,' Camilla frowned.

'Please stay, Camilla,' she pleaded.

The other woman shook her head. 'I think it would be better if I left. I'd like to say it's been nice talking to you, Mr Anderson,' she sounded upset. 'But if what Chelsea says is true I don't think it has been.'

'It has,' he told her firmly, pointedly, turning to Chelsea once they were alone. 'I've been trying to talk to you for the last week.'

'I believe Lucas's housekeeper told you I didn't want to talk to you,' she said stiffly.

'Yes,' he nodded. 'And I could understand that. But I just wanted to apologise——'

'You think an apology makes everything all right again?' she cut in disbelievingly. 'You wrote a story that was completely erroneous——'

'I didn't write the story that appeared in the newspaper,' he shook his head.

'Lucas telephoned the newspaper,' she told him with distaste for his lie. 'They freely admitted that their informant was a John Anderson.'

'Informant,' he nodded. 'They took the story I submitted and turned it into—into what you saw,' he grimaced. 'I swear to you that I didn't write what they printed.'

'It doesn't really matter now who wrote it, does it,' she dismissed wearily. 'The damage has been done, both to Lucas and myself.'

'I know,' he sighed. 'And I'm sorry. You've

already had to face so much, that story on top of everything else must have really distressed you.'

Chelsea took compassion on him, some of her anger fading; he did genuinely seem upset. 'It didn't help matters,' she conceded. 'And I can tell you, Lucas was absolutely furious about it.'

'I'm sure,' John nodded, chewing on his bottom lip. 'I couldn't believe my luck when I ran into you the way I did. I was following up a very sketchy lead a friend of mine in the States had given me, and when you got into the lift I recognised you immediately from your photographs.'

'You deliberately coaxed that information out of me,' she reminded coldly.

'So that I could write a humane story,' he insisted. 'Not something full of sketchy facts and innuendo! I was as disgusted by what they did print as you must have been.'

'Is that why you've come here under false pretences this morning and tried to get information out of Camilla?' she accused.

He shook his head. 'I didn't ask her anything, and she didn't tell me anything. And even if she had I wouldn't write about it; I owe you that at least for what happened last week. I really am sorry, Chelsea,' he said softly. 'I'll leave now that I've had the chance to tell you that. And you won't hear from me again, I can assure you of that.'

'Not even in tomorrow's newspapers?' she said sceptically, having learnt the hard way to distrust this man.

'No.' His mouth twisted ruefully. 'I like you, Chelsea, I never meant to hurt you,' he added seriously. 'I promise you that I'll write no more about you or your family.'

'That isn't a very professional attitude,' she mocked.

He grimaced. 'To tell you the truth this last week has shaken me up a bit. I work for a local newspaper back home where the highlight of the week is the latest missing cat escapade; I'd never before dealt with a story as big as this one. It's a cut-throat business on Fleet Street, and I don't think I'm up to it yet, maybe I never will be. I'm going back home, anyway, and I'm not sure I'll ever be back.'

Chelsea couldn't help but smile. 'Maybe you just jumped in to too big a story.'

'Maybe,' he shrugged. 'But I certainly don't intend to let this happen to me again. Now I'd better leave you in peace,' he gave a rueful smile as he moved to the door. 'Thank you for hearing me out, I hope one day you'll be able to forgive me.'

He was so sincere that she couldn't help but believe his regret was genuine. 'I already have,' she said with her usual warmth.

He gave a rueful smile. 'Thanks for being so understanding.'

She may have been, but she had a feeling that understanding was the last thing Lucas was going to feel, that he was going to be furiously angry when he heard John Anderson had managed to talk to her a second time!

CHAPTER EIGHT

SHE was right, he was.

Maybe she should have warned Camilla against telling Lucas of John's visit, but the other woman unwittingly revealed that he had been to the apartment as the three of them retired to the lounge after dinner.

Lucas grew very still, his jaw rigid. 'Anderson came here?' he rasped.

'Well, yes,' Chelsea blushed. 'But——'

'You actually let him in here after what happened last time you spoke to him?' Lucas thundered.

'No, I——'

'Don't tell me you met him in the lift again,' he dismissed disgustedly.

'You're being unfair——'

'Unfair!' he repeated incredulously. 'You invite some damned reporter here when he's already told the whole country we're lovers and you call me unfair! Oh yes,' he insisted grimly as Camilla gasped, very pale beneath the perfection of her make-up, unable to conceal the dark smudges of unhappiness beneath her eyes. 'That's exactly what he did,' he ground out. 'And Chelsea actually invited him into my home!'

'I didn't——'

'It was me, Lucas,' Camilla told him quietly.

'Don't try and protect her, Camilla,' he sighed impatiently. 'It seems to me that she's been protected by one person or another all her life, and it's time that it stopped.' He towered over

Chelsea like some avenging angel. 'If Anderson reports one libellous statement about me or a member of my family you'll find yourself sued along with him!'

'Lucas!' Camilla gasped.

'Do I make myself clear?' he ignored his sister's shocked reaction, glaring at Chelsea.

'You make yourself very clear,' she nodded abruptly.

'Lucas, it *was* me,' Camilla insisted. 'I had no idea who he was, and I invited him in.'

'I don't believe you,' he shook his head. 'Chelsea has been behaving irresponsibly, one way or another, since the moment she arrived here. It's time she faced her responsibilities——'

'Lucas, will you please listen to me,' Camilla raised her voice impatiently. 'I *did* let John Anderson in here. In fact, I brought him up to the apartment after my walk. I thought he was a friend of Chelsea's, he acted as if he were.'

Lucas grew very still, looking at his sister with narrowed eyes. 'Is that the truth?'

'Of course it is,' she snapped. 'And stop glowering at me, I'm not a nineteen-year-old that you think you can browbeat!'

He glared at her. 'Sometimes you act like one!' He slammed out of the room.

'What a dear brother I have,' Camilla said with sweet sarcasm.

'Why is he *like* that?' Chelsea flared. 'Is it just that he can't bear to be wrong?'

Camilla smiled at her anger. 'No one likes to be wrong,' she drawled. 'And arrogantly decisive men even less so than most.' She frowned. 'But I have to admit that he's even more unreasonable than usual at the moment.'

'Why?'

Camilla shrugged. 'I think maybe you're making him realise what he's lost.'

Now Chelsea was totally confused, and said so. 'Lucas seems to have everything,' she added.

'Looks can be deceptive. I'm sure that part of the problem is that Lucas can see himself in you at that age——'

'You heard him,' Chelsea derided. 'He thinks I'm irresponsible. Lucas was *never* irresponsible,' she said bitterly.

Camilla gave her a sympathetic smile. 'Lucas was wild at your age——'

'Lucas was? I don't believe it!'

'But he was,' the other woman insisted. 'Our parents were—repressive——'

'He told me,' she nodded.

'He did?' Camilla said with slow consideration. 'Now that's interesting. Anyway, in his late teens Lucas rebelled——'

'He said *you* were the rebellious one.'

Camilla smiled. 'Nothing like Lucas, believe me. He even ran off to live in a commune for a time.'

She somehow couldn't imagine Lucas as a 'free-spirited' person. 'What went wrong?' she grimaced.

Camilla laughed. 'My father would have said what went right!' She sobered, shrugging. 'He grew up, I suppose. He came home, repressed his own ambitions and entered the law like our father wanted him to.'

'I thought Lucas had always wanted to be a lawyer,' she frowned.

The other woman shook her head. 'He can write. At least, he used to,' she shrugged. 'I haven't known him do anything like that for a long time.'

'You mean books and things?' she was stunned.

Camilla nodded. 'He's good too.'

'Has he ever had anything published?'

'He's never sent any of his work to a publisher,' Camilla sighed. 'And just lately he's become too immersed in his career to have time for his writing. Jennifer Sutton doesn't help, she's so ambitious she encourages Lucas to live for his career too.'

'He isn't seeing her anymore,' Chelsea told her quietly. 'At least, he wasn't a couple of days ago. They had this big argument——'

'Jennifer and Lucas did?' Camilla sounded incredulous.

She blushed as she remembered the scene that had followed the argument. 'Miss Sutton took exception to my staying here with Lucas.'

'And he took exception to her saying so,' Camilla said knowingly. 'I bet Jennifer was surprised when he took your part; I think she had designs on being Mrs Lucas McAdams.'

'Maybe she still will be.' She shrugged to hide the pain she felt at the thought. 'After all, they still work together,' she added almost questioningly, wanting Camilla's verbal assurance that she didn't think Lucas would return to the other woman.

'Maybe,' Camilla agreed dismissively. 'I think I'll go to bed now.' She stood up.

'I'll be through in a few minutes,' Chelsea nodded distractedly.

'Don't rush to bed on my account,' Camilla told her. 'I'm going to take a couple of pills tonight to ensure that I get some sleep.'

'I promise not to tell Lucas,' she mocked. 'He doesn't approve, you know.'

Camilla grimaced. 'My dear brother is far too

opinionated. Thank goodness I stopped listening to him years ago!'

Chelsea's smile faded as soon as the other woman had left. Lucas was opinionated, he was also overbearing, bossy, and obstinate—and she still loved him! He was impossible to reason with, so firm in his beliefs that he couldn't even begin to accept it when he was wrong.

'Has Camilla gone to bed?'

She turned sharply at the softly spoken question, Lucas having discarded the jacket to his suit, the white shirt partly unbuttoned down his chest, his dark hair slightly ruffled, as if he had been running his fingers through it. 'Er—yes,' she answered him, unsure of his mood. 'She went through several minutes ago.'

'Damn,' he muttered. 'Oh well, I may as well apologise to you now and talk to Camilla in the morning.'

'A . . . apologise?' she echoed dazedly.

His mouth twisted. 'Don't look so surprised, I am capable of admitting it when I'm in the wrong.'

And she and Camilla had just decided he wasn't! Some of what she was thinking must have shown in her face because Lucas's mouth tightened angrily.

'You obviously disagree,' he rasped.

'No, I——'

'I couldn't think of any other way than at your invitation Anderson could have got in here. I had no idea Camilla would be so stupid——'

'You're spoiling the apology now,' she rebuked.

'All right,' he sighed. 'So *gullible* as to be taken in by the apparent innocence of a member of the press.'

'But John is innocent,' she protested. 'He only wanted to apologise for the story that appeared in the newspaper, it was taken out of his hands.'

'He told you that?'

'Yes.'

'And you believed him?'

She blushed at his derision. 'Yes, I believed him!'

'Enough to reveal a few more family confidences?' Lucas scorned.

'God, why are you such an arrogant——'

'Yes?' he prompted tautly as she halted abruptly.

'Bastard,' she finished forcefully, goaded beyond endurance.

His mouth twisted. 'I think my parents might have something to say about that,' he derided.

'From the sound of it your parents have already had too much say in your life!'

Lucas looked at her probingly. 'And just what do you mean by that?'

'Camilla told me you didn't want to be a lawyer at all,' she challenged. 'That you can write.'

'She had no right——'

'She knows I love you.'

'God, do you tell everyone you talk to?' he demanded irritably. 'Did you tell Anderson too?' he frowned.

'No——'

'Thank God you had that much sense at least!'

'You've misjudged him as you misjudge everyone else,' she snapped agitatedly. 'He went to the newspaper with that story, yes, but they didn't print what he wrote. It was their idea to make it look as if our living together was more than it was.'

Lucas shook his head pityingly. 'You're very naive.'

'And you're very pig-headed!'

'Careful, Chelsea, your compliments might go to my head,' he derided.

She sighed as she realised how heated their argument was becoming. 'Why do you have to be so suspicious of everyone?'

'It comes along with the job.'

'A job you hate!'

'I don't hate it at all, Chelsea,' he told her grimly. 'Without being immodest, I know I'm good at it, and no one can hate something they're good at.'

'But what did you sacrifice to be good at it?' she persisted. 'If you can write then that's what you should be doing.'

'Who says I can write,' he dismissed abruptly.

'Camilla does. And so do I,' she added challengingly.

Lucas gave her a pitying look. 'You've never seen any of my work.'

'I know *you*,' she told him softly. 'And I know you would never contemplate doing something you aren't good at.'

'You really are infatuated, aren't you,' he scorned dismissively.

'I'm in love,' she corrected quietly. 'And I have an idea,' she added eagerly.

'Yes?' he prompted warily.

'Don't look so worried,' she smiled at his expression. 'You're convinced that John only came here today to get another story, right?'

'Right,' he nodded.

'Which means we should be on the front page of a newspaper again tomorrow?'

'Probably,' he said slowly.

'There's no probably about it,' she insisted impatiently. 'If John is the hardened reporter you say he is then he'll certainly make a story about Camilla being here with us now. And if he does then you are right, I am a naive fool.'

'And if he doesn't?' Lucas prompted warily.

'You let me see some of your writing,' she announced happily, pleased with her plan.

'No!'

'Why not?' she pleaded.

'Because I don't intend leaving myself open to your ridicule,' he rasped. 'You have no qualifications to say if my work is good or bad.'

At least he had admitted that he still had some of his work! 'I'm an avid reader, surely that qualifies me?'

'I write murder-mysteries——'

'My favourite,' she said with relish.

'Chelsea——'

'What have you really got to lose, Lucas?' she persisted forcefully. 'I thought you were so confident you would win?' she taunted.

'I will,' he nodded grimly.

'Then make the deal,' Chelsea prompted.

'I haven't written anything in years——'

'That's okay,' she dismissed this excuse. 'I enjoy period murder-mysteries most of all!'

'You little——'

'You're the one that keeps going on about the age difference,' she reminded innocently.

Lucas heaved a defeated sigh. 'All right, it's a deal. As you say, I'm going to win anyway.'

She was waiting for him when he arrived home from work the next evening, her hands held out expectantly as he scowled at her. John hadn't let her down, not a single word had been printed about them, in any newspaper. And Lucas had seen the newspapers before he left for work that morning, she had checked with Mrs Harvey, so he had had all day to resign himself to the fact that she had won the deal, that he had to hand over one of his manuscripts this evening for her to read.

'Can't you at least wait until after dinner?' he glowered at her beaming face.

'I'll eat later,' she dismissed.

He gave an irritated sigh. 'I'm sure I wouldn't have been so—so gleeful if I'd won!'

She grinned. 'You would have been impossible! Go get the manuscript, Lucas,' she encouraged.

'Oh to hell with it!' He turned on his heel and left the room, returning minutes later with a folder in his hands. 'Just don't expect too much.' He strode across the room to pour himself a drink. 'Where's Camilla?'

'Visiting an old schoolfriend,' she answered in a preoccupied voice, itching to read the manuscript he had guarded so possessively.

'Heather Manning,' he guessed correctly. 'She always goes to see her when she's troubled.'

Chelsea frowned. 'Have you found out what's bothering her yet; she won't talk to me about it.'

He shrugged dismissively. 'It's really none of our business, is it,' he told her cuttingly.

She flushed. 'I'll see you later,' she told him tightly.

'Don't rush,' he called after her mockingly.

She had no intention of rushing, but from the first page of the neatly typed manuscript she was captivated by the intricacies of the characters Lucas had masterminded, each new twist to the story coming as a complete surprise to her.

After two engrossed hours she had reached the last grippingly exciting page, gasping as she finally discovered who the murderer was, and the reasons behind his actions. It was a fantastic story, was surely destined for the bestseller list, could even be made into a movie. Then why hadn't Lucas sent it to a publisher as he obviously should have done, he couldn't be blind to his own talent?

He looked up from the newspaper he was reading, his mouth twisting derisively at her frowning expression. 'That bad, hm?'

'It's—it's——'

'Speechless, hm?' he mocked hardly, standing up to take the manuscript from her reluctant fingers.

He really didn't know how good he was! 'It's so well written that if you don't send it to a publisher then I'll sneak into your bedroom in the middle of the night and send it to them myself!' she told him fervently.

'Believe me,' he taunted. 'If you sneaked into my bedroom in the middle of the night the manuscript wouldn't be the only thing you would get!'

She knew his mockery hid pleasure in her praise, that although he appeared very self-confident that he needed it as much as the next man. 'Promise?' she said huskily.

He smiled dismissively. 'I'm glad you enjoyed the story, Chelsea, but it's very amateurish——'

'It's fantastic!'

'Says you,' he said condescendingly.

'What is it with you?' she flared angrily. 'Why can't you take and accept praise? A psychiatrist would have great fun in your head!'

'A *psychiatrist*?' Lucas thundered predictably. 'I can assure you I don't have a problem——'

'Oh yes you do,' she insisted goadingly.

Lucas's eyes narrowed at the air of expectancy

that surrounded her. 'What are you up to now?' he asked slowly.

She grimaced her disappointment. 'Well, in all the good books this should be the point where you get angry enough with me to forcefully make love to me!'

'Did it happen in mine?'

'No . . .'

'Then it can't be a good book, can it?' he taunted triumphantly.

Chelsea sighed at his manipulation of the conversation. 'Then you aren't going to make love to me?'

'I don't think that would be a good idea——'

'What does your body say?'

'My body . . .?'

'Mm, what does it say?'

He frowned. 'My body doesn't usually talk to me,' he drawled mockingly, evading a direct answer.

She gave an impatient sigh. 'I suppose *I* could always get mad enough to forcefully make love to *you*,' she muttered.

Lucas grinned at the idea. 'You could try.'

'I could?'

His mouth quirked. 'I said you could *try*, Chelsea,' he taunted. 'You won't succeed. Unfortunately, for you, you're going to need my co-operation.'

'And you won't give it?' she arched light brows.

'No,' he confirmed tightly, his amusement over the situation fading at the light of challenge in her eyes.

'Go and put your manuscript away and then come back here,' she instructed determinedly.

'Chelsea——'

'Unless you're scared to?' she challenged.

'Don't play these games with me, Chelsea,' he warned.

'Why not?' she dismissed. 'You're so confident I'm going to be wrong—again,' she added pointedly.

His mouth tightened at the challenge in her tone. 'I'll be back in a few minutes.'

Chelsea took advantage of his absence to lower the lighting and turn on the flame to the artificially realistic fire. If she were going to try and seduce him she may as well set the scene! She also threw the cushions off the sofa on to the floor, she was in the process of pouring them both a glass of wine when Lucas came back into the room. His eyes narrowed warily as he took in the scene she had deliberately created.

'This is the way it's done, isn't it?' She made herself comfortable on the cushions, holding up his glass of wine invitingly. 'I watch a lot of movies,' she explained smilingly.

'The wrong sort, by the look of this,' Lucas muttered as he sank down next to her on the cushions, taking the glass of wine, careful not to touch her as he did so. 'You forgot something. Music,' he reminded at her questioning look. 'There's always romantic music in the background during scenes like these in films.'

'I'd prefer it if we made our own.' She took the glass out of his hand and put it down on the table with her own.

'If I'd used that line you would have accused me of being corny,' he teased.

She shook her head. 'If you had used that line I would have fallen straight into your arms. As it is,' she draped herself decorously across his knees, her arms up about his neck as she slowly pulled him down to her, 'I intend having you fall into mine.'

His arms moved to support her as she brought their lips into contact, moving her mouth caressingly against his. His lips remained coldly unmoving, his arms loose about her.

Chelsea increased her efforts to gain a response from him, moving the tip of her tongue against those cool lips, feeling a momentary tension in his body before he slowly relaxed again. That uncontrollable response to her gave her hope, and her hands moved slowly to the buttons of his shirt.

'What do you think you're doing?' Lucas rasped, his expression grim.

She looked at him with widely innocent eyes. 'If I were the man then this is what he would be doing.' She continued to unbutton his shirt.

'That's enough!' His hand clamped over hers as she moved to touch him beneath the silk of his shirt. 'This has gone far enough,' he rasped. 'It should never have begun.' He put Chelsea away from him so that she lay back among the cushions, her mouth red and pouting, her breasts thrusting against the softness of her blouse. It was here that Lucas's gaze locked. 'Do you have anything on under that?'

Puzzlement flickered in her eyes. 'Just a camisole. A brown lace one,' she added breathlessly as his eyes suddenly glowed like twin black coals.

He swallowed hard before slowly following her down among the cushions. 'Chelsea . . .!'

Her arms welcomed him as he lay above her, her lips parted to meet the heat of his, her response instantaneous as his tongue thrust hotly into her mouth, meeting that thrust with some of her own, hearing his groan low in his throat.

His fingers were much more expert on the buttons of her blouse than hers had been on his shirt, the garment stripped from her body within seconds, his eyes very dark on the revealing camisole and the twin peaks beneath it.

'Kiss me, Lucas!' she groaned achingly.

His mouth didn't return to hers as she pleaded for him to do, but sucked a nipple through the silky material, his tongue a soft sensuous rasp against the silk. Her other nipple instantly swelled for the same loving touch, not disappointed as he left the material clinging damply to the pampered breast to lovingly caress the neglected one.

Heat surged through her body at the eroticism of the caress, gasping her aching pleasure as he took the nipple fully into the warm cavern of his mouth, pulling on it with a pleasure-pain that made her fingers dig like tallons into the tautness of his back.

Her expression was bereft as he moved up and away from her, throwing the cushions haphazardly back on to the sofa. 'Lucas, please . . .!' she groaned her need in the face of his rejection. 'Please!'

He bent to sweep her up into his arms, pausing to fiercely claim her passion-swollen lips. 'I am going to please you, my love,' he rasped. 'You're going to get your wish. But not here on the floor where Camilla could walk in on us at any moment. We're going to my bedroom.'

'I love you,' she groaned.

He made no reply to the admission, moving powerfully to his bedroom, pulling back the covers to lay her down on the sheet, his gaze never leaving hers as he hurriedly stripped the clothes from his body. Chelsea watched him with languorous eyes, trembling with longing once he stood naked in front of her, groaning as she imagined the beauty of his body joined with her own.

He removed her own clothes at a much more leisurely pace, not leaving an inch of her flesh untouched by the warm moisture of his mouth as he did so, Chelsea burning with a passion that threatened to erupt out of control at any moment, although Lucas seemed to know that too, stopping before she could topple over the edge into sensual oblivion.

'Will you touch me?' he rasped throatily. 'Let me know the touch of your soft milky-white hands?'

She did look very pale against his darker skin, loving the feel of his hard flesh, guided by instinct in her lack of experience, satisfied with her effort as Lucas gasped his own spiralling pleasure, his body tense as he fought for control.

Finally he moved to pin her beneath him on the bed, his eyes full of flames as he gazed down at her wanton beauty. 'Do you trust me?' he asked raggedly.

'I love you,' she told him, as if that said everything.

'I'll try not to hurt you,' he promised as he lay between her parted thighs, moving in erotic rhythm against her as his mouth claimed hers but his thrusting thighs didn't.

Chelsea could feel herself becoming increasingly moist for him as the hardness of his desire continued to move against her, promising and tempting and yet denying her that final possession that she craved.

'Please, Lucas,' she pleaded on a sob when she could stand no more of this torture. 'Please *now!*'

'Not yet,' he shook his head. 'I don't want to hurt you.'

'You won't,' she begged, in the grip of a mindless desire.

Still he didn't possess her, kissing her deeply, penetratingly, with a promise of things to come.

Chelsea knew as he claimed her that he had been right to prolong this moment for as long as possible, still feeling a little pain as he moved surely inside her, although it was soon forgotten as his body moved in hers in a quickly rising rhythm.

As she gasped her fiery release she felt Lucas tense and harden, groaning his own shuddering release as he buried his face in her throat.

'I love you, Lucas. I love you,' she told him over and over again, a long time returning from that pleasure-filled plateau he had taken her to.

His breathing was a long time steadying, still erratic as he finally leant on his elbows to look down at her. 'I wish I could tell you the same thing,' he rasped. 'But I don't know what I feel for you.' He shook his head. 'I do know I could become physically enthralled by you; what happened between us just now was the most incredibly earth-shattering experience of my entire life!'

Knowing the sort of man he was, a man who couldn't admit to any weakness, Chelsea knew what this admission cost him. And she had been wrong about him remaining coldly aloof even during lovemaking; with his tousled dark hair and passion-darkened eyes he looked as shaken as she felt.

'It's enough,' she assured him, lovingly

touching the hair at his nape. 'It's more than enough,' she gasped as she felt him hardening inside her.

Some time during the lengthy loving she was aware of the apartment door closing, the door across the hall from this one closing seconds later; Camilla was home!

But she thought only fleetingly of the other woman's presence in the apartment as Lucas took her to that plateau again, the passion longer and even more intense this time, Chelsea shaking as she clung to the dampness of his shoulders.

'I should go back to my own room,' she finally said regretfully, reluctant to leave the man she loved now more than ever.

Lucas lay beside her, his cheek against her breasts as she held him to her. 'You aren't going anywhere,' he told her arrogantly.

'But Camilla——'

'I only said I didn't want her to walk in on us; she's a grown woman, old enough to understand our being together like this.'

Chelsea gave a contented sigh, snuggling closer against him, asleep within minutes.

She woke what seemed seconds later to the sound of raised voices somewhere in the apartment, frowning her confusion as she saw Lucas still lay beside her asleep, his arm possessively about her waist.

But he too jerked awake as the voices became louder. 'What the hell——!' He blinked to clear the sleep from his mind, sitting up. 'What's going on?' he frowned.

She shook her head. 'I have no idea. The shouting woke me up too.' She watched as Lucas hurriedly pulled on his clothes, her own movements slower as she put on his bathrobe, her body now feeling the effects of its previously unknown possession by any man, let alone a man who was as passionately experienced as Lucas was.

'Maybe you should stay here,' he warned in a concerned voice as he saw she intended following him from the room.

'I'm coming with you,' she told him firmly. If Camilla had surprised burglars in the apartment then she didn't intend letting Lucas go out there and face them alone.

She followed his stealthy movements from the bedroom, gasping as they entered the lounge together to find her father and Camilla were the ones shouting at each other!

CHAPTER NINE

'JACE!' Her cried greeting was a mixture of surprise and puzzlement, surprise that her father was here at all when he hadn't let anyone know he was coming, puzzlement that he should be arguing with Camilla in this way; to her knowledge he and Camilla never argued!

'Princess.' Jace held out his arms to her, and she was shocked at how thin and drawn he looked, deep lines of tiredness etched into his face.

'I've been so worried about you.' And with good reason, she realised as she hugged him. 'Why didn't you tell us you were coming?' she demanded to know.

He looked past her to Camilla. 'I——'

'He told me, Chelsea,' the other woman admitted reluctantly. 'I—I forgot to tell you.'

'Camilla?' Lucas's tone was reproving.

'It slipped my mind.' Her gaze flashed defiantly as she defended herself.

'I would have been here earlier,' Jace cut in softly, Chelsea still held securely at his side. 'But the flight was delayed, and then I had to check myself into a hotel.' He looked down at Chelsea with questioning eyes. 'I seem to have caught everyone in bed.'

The hot colour flooded her cheeks, and although she hadn't seen herself in a mirror she felt sure her lips must be red and swollen from Lucas's kisses, that her eyes were languorous from the passion they had shared. And most damning of all, she was wearing Lucas's bathrobe and obviously nothing else!

'Jace, I think I should explain——'

'No need, Lucas,' the older man cut in firmly. 'Chelsea is a little too old, and knows me too well, for me to start lecturing her at this late stage. And you happen to be the best friend I ever had. I'm pleased, whatever there is between the two of you.'

Chelsea could see that Lucas was far from pleased about any of this situation!

'Nevertheless, we'll talk about this in the morning,' he insisted grimly. 'But right now I suggest we all get some sleep. You look tired, Jace, and—things, might not seem so complicated then.'

'If by "things" you mean me,' Camilla snapped angrily. 'Then let me tell you *nothing* will have changed by tomorrow!' She stormed from the room, her bedroom door closing seconds later.

'Despite what she said, I'm sure she'll be calmer by the morning,' Lucas assured the other man.

Jace suddenly looked old, every single one of his forty-five years. 'If I leave here now she'll be gone by the morning,' he said heavily. 'I realise that my family descending on you in this way must be inconveniencing you, Lucas, besides overcrowding you, but I'd like to spend the night here if that's okay. This sofa looks as if it might be comfortable——'

'It is,' Lucas nodded grimly. 'And I'll be using it. You can use my bedroom——'

'I wouldn't hear of it,' Jace refused. 'I've slept in worse places than this couch, believe me,' he gave a humourless smile. 'But right now I think

I'd better have a word with my puzzled daughter.'
Warmth entered his eyes as he looked down at
her.

To say she was puzzled was an understatement;
she had no idea what was going on!

Lucas nodded abruptly. 'I'll see you both in
the morning.'

'Lucas?' she prompted sharply.

His mouth tightened at the hurt in her face.
'We'll talk then too,' he told her firmly.

'But——'

'Like he said, Princess.' Jace's arm tightened
about her warningly. 'A lot of things will seem
different in the morning, much less complicated,'
he added assuringly.

Lucas's mouth was tight. 'I'll just get your
bed-linen,' he told the other man.

'He's more than a little embarrassed, Princess,'
Jace told her regretfully once they were alone.
'Give him a chance to get used to the idea that
after finally succumbing to your—charms, your
father arrived on the scene.' He gave a rueful
smile. 'Tonight *was* the first time this happened,
wasn't it?'

'Yes,' she confirmed huskily. 'But how did you
know that?'

He shrugged broad shoulders. 'Lucas's attitude. I'm just sorry I interrupted.'

'Oh but you didn't—I mean,' she blushed her
embarrassment. 'We were asleep when you
arrived,' she admitted awkwardly. 'I——' she
broke off as Lucas strode back into the room with
the bed-linen, looking at them both with
narrowed eyes before going back to his bedroom.
'Poor Lucas,' she groaned. 'He has the look of a
hunted man.'

Jace sank down wearily in an armchair while

she made up the sofa into a bed for him. 'From what you told me on the telephone he's looked like that for some time!'

'Maybe,' she grimaced, sitting down on the bed. 'What's wrong between you and Camilla? And don't say nothing,' she warned. 'Because I've never known Camilla to act or talk the way that she did tonight.'

He leant back with his eyes closed. 'Neither have I,' he admitted flatly. 'I thought she might have calmed down the last few days, but nothing has changed.'

Chelsea frowned. 'Do you love her?'

'Chelsea——'

'Jace,' she prompted lovingly.

'Yes, I love her, I love her very much,' he admitted with a heavy sigh.

'And does she love you?'

'I thought so.' He shook his head. 'But now I'm not so sure.'

'*I'm* sure that she does,' Chelsea told him firmly.

His eyes were still closed. 'There are too many complications,' he muttered.

'And am I one of them?' she asked anxiously.

'You were,' he acknowledged.

'But not now?'

He sighed. 'I don't think so. I don't know. God, I'm so tired,' he groaned. 'I don't seem to have slept for days!' His eyes were bloodshot as he looked at her.

'I don't think you have,' she stood up. 'This conversation can wait until tomorrow too,' she told him gently, bending to kiss and hug him. 'Get some sleep now.'

'Princess,' he stopped her at the door.

'Yes?' she frowned her concern.

He smiled. 'I love you.'

She smiled her relief that that was all he was going to say. 'I love you too.'

She hesitated when she reached the door of the bedroom she had been sharing with Camilla, turning determinedly to the door opposite, entering quietly, walking over to the side of the bed, looking down at Lucas with hungry eyes. He lay on his back, his chest bare, one arm draped across his eyes, the even tenor of his breathing seeming to indicate sleep. Seeming to. As she continued to stand there she noticed the tenor changing, becoming more ragged, tension about his mouth.

'I came to return this,' she spoke quietly, laying the discarded robe across the foot of his bed. 'Good night, Lucas.'

His arm fell from his eyes as he sat up in bed, looking hungrily at her nakedness. 'Damn you,' he muttered aggressively before pulling her down beside him, one bare hair-roughened leg covering the lower half of her body and pinning her to the bed. 'You shouldn't have come here,' he said gruffly.

Her arms curved about his neck. 'I love you, Lucas.'

He groaned, his mouth descending to hers with fierce possession, demanding her response rather than seducing her to it as he had on the last two occasions they had made love, thrusting into her with a fierceness that took her breath away—and then gave her so much pleasure that she hurt him in return, her nails digging into his buttocks before he groaned to a shuddering climax with her and fell damply against her.

'Still think I should have stayed away?' she teased lovingly.

'No,' he admitted shakily. 'But you can't stay here.'

'Why can't I?' she frowned.

Lucas leant on his elbows to look down at her. 'Because your father is out in the lounge.'

'That didn't stop you just now,' she reminded.

'No,' he acknowledged with a sigh. 'But can't you see I'm having trouble coping with this situation. I've never slept with a woman before knowing her father was in the next room!'

'Jace is very broad-minded——'

'But I'm not,' he said grimly, levering away from her, a spasm of lingering pleasure crossing his face as he did so.

'Jace once told me that you should never make love with a person if you can't wake up next to them in the morning and feel good about it.'

Lucas nodded. 'Your father gave you some very good advice.'

She blinked back the tears. 'How do *you* feel about waking up next to me in the morning?'

His eyes were hooded. 'You aren't staying the night,' he told her firmly.

'I see.' She got out of bed. 'Then I guess I have my answer, don't I. You really meant it when you said you didn't want to be involved with me!'

'Chelsea——'

'I'll have to borrow your bathrobe again, I'm sorry,' she pulled it on with shaking fingers. 'I'm also sorry I forced you into this.'

'You didn't force me into anything.' He jumped out of bed, looking like a long-legged god. 'I just don't feel right sharing a bed with you when your father is in the apartment.' He grasped her arms to turn her to face him. 'Try to understand, Chelsea——'

'Oh, I do.' She pulled away from him, the shimmer of tears in her eyes making him look a blur. 'And maybe I wouldn't have liked waking up next to you either! You probably have a heavy stubble, and—and——' She couldn't go on, her voice breaking emotionally, knowing that when morning came she would love him as much as ever, stubble and all. 'Excuse me,' she wrenched out of his arms, running from the room.

Lucas didn't attempt to follow her, as she had known he wouldn't, taking several minutes to calm herself before quietly entering the bedroom she shared with Camilla. The first thing she saw as she entered the room was her blouse lying across her bed. Camilla had obviously picked it up and lain it there when she came in, had known that her brother and Chelsea were in his room together!

Chelsea held the blouse to her as she sat on the side of the bed and cried. Lucas hadn't cared that his sister knew of the two of them being together, so he must just be using Jace as an excuse! She had made a fool of herself, had forced herself on him. And yet she still loved him.

And her crying must be disturbing Camilla. She turned guiltily to the other woman's bed, gasping as she noticed for the first time that the bedclothes were thrown back and that Camilla had gone.

Could the other woman have left the apartment after all, be so determined not to talk to Jace that she had crept out without any of them realising it?

Well, Jace had to be told. Maybe he would even be able to catch up with the other woman that way. Chelsea rushed out of the room and into the lounge, only to come to an abrupt halt.

Camilla hadn't left at all, was closely entwined with Jace on the sofa as they both slept!

It would be silly for Chelsea to deny that it felt strange to see her father in bed with any other woman but her mother; it felt very strange indeed. But even as she watched them, her gaze riveted, Camilla snuggled even closer to Jace, her mumbled words completely distinguishable as she told him how much she loved him.

Chelsea felt shaken as she returned to her room. It was just so weird to see Jace and Camilla together; before tonight she had never even suspected they were more than just friends. But as long as Jace was happy, as long as he lost that tired look of defeat that was so alien to him, she was pleased for them.

Her own sleep was much more disturbed as she tried not to think of facing Lucas again. She already felt humiliated enough.

When she woke in the morning Camilla was in the single bed across from her, the gentle smile on her lips indicative of the fact that whatever problems she and Jace had had they were straightened out now.

It was still early when she crept from her own bed, badly in need of a cup of coffee, smiling when she saw she wasn't the only one in need of that early morning shot of caffeine.

'Is there enough in the pot for two?' she greeted her father lightly.

He turned to smile at her, looking much better than when he had arrived the previous evening, the teasing sparkle back in his eyes, the vitality in his movements. 'I'll get it for you,' he stood up, lean and handsome in fitted denims and a dark blue shirt.

She shook her head. 'I can get it,' she insisted,

doing so, sitting on the kitchen chair opposite him. 'You're looking better today.'

Some of the laughter left his eyes. 'You aren't,' he said quietly.

She shrugged dismissively. 'I'm fine.'

'Are you?'

She couldn't stop the colour entering her cheeks, or the bitterness in her voice. 'A little older, a lot wiser,' she grimaced. 'But I'll survive.'

Jace looked puzzled. 'Did you see Lucas again last night after we talked?'

'Yes,' she confirmed bluntly.

'That wasn't a wise move, Princess.'

'No,' she acknowledged curtly. 'But at least now I really know how he feels about me.'

'And how is that?' Jace prompted softly.

She shrugged. 'As okay for the odd evening in bed, but——' she swallowed hard, forcing control into her voice. Her head went back proudly. 'He wouldn't want to wake up next to me in the morning, and he certainly wouldn't feel good about it—to use one of your own quotes!'

'Princess——'

'Don't look so worried, Jace,' she cajoled lightly. 'I told you, I'll get over it. Once I leave here I'll never have to see him again, and——'

'I wouldn't count on that, Princess,' Jace grimaced.

She looked at him sharply, tensing. 'What do you mean?'

He gave a deep sigh. 'There's something I've been meaning to tell you for some time, I started to explain last night, but I was tired, and it could have come out all wrong.'

She gave him an understanding smile. 'You told me you love Camilla.'

He nodded. 'There's more to it than that.'

'I think you should know that when I returned to my bedroom last night Camilla wasn't there,' Chelsea told him softly. 'I knew you desperately wanted to talk to her today, so I came to tell you she had gone.'

'You saw us together?' His eyes were narrowed.

'Yes.'

He sighed. 'There's more to it than even that. You see——'

'More?' she exclaimed. 'How can there be more?'

Jace pulled a face. 'I knew I should have told you sooner, that you should have been there, but—well—Camilla and I were married a month ago!' He watched her anxiously after making the announcement.

Chelsea paled. *Married!* She hadn't even suspected that things had gone that far.

'We've been in love a very long time, and last month I finally persuaded Camilla to marry me,' Jace continued raggedly.

Last month. Lucas said he had been in Los Angeles visiting Jace last month. 'Lucas knew about this.' It was a statement, not a question.

'Yes,' her father confirmed heavily.

'He was at the wedding.'

'He was one of our witnesses,' Jace nodded. 'Princess, there are such a lot of other things I have to tell you, to explain——'

'And I want to hear them, really I do,' she told him numbly, standing up. 'But I'm not feeling very receptive right now. I—I have to go out.'

'Princess . . .!'

'We'll talk when I get back,' she assured him before running from the room, quietly entering the bedroom to collect her jacket; Camilla was still asleep.

So many things made sense now, Jace sending her to Lucas in the first place, Lucas's acceptance of that visit, the time he had said she was almost a member of his family. God, Jace's marriage to Camilla made Lucas her step-uncle! How ironic when he had told Jennifer he felt like her uncle. Had the other woman known of the marriage too? She had a feeling that she had. Only Chelsea had been considered too juvenile to accept the marriage.

Jace had been wrong to keep such a thing from her, although she accepted that the last few weeks he had had a lot of other things on his mind, but she had been with Lucas constantly the last two weeks, and still he hadn't mentioned his sister's marriage to her father. So much for their agreement that there would be honesty between them! Lucas didn't——

'Chelsea!'

She turned sharply as Lucas softly spoke her name, looking at him coldly. He looked as if he had dressed in a hurry, his shirt not quite tucked into his trousers, his hair only vaguely tidy. 'Did you oversleep, Lucas?' she said contemptuously, knowing he was usually up and dressed by the seven-fifteen it was now.

His mouth tightened. 'Let's go outside.' He looked pointedly at Camilla as she slept on. 'I want to talk to you.'

'And I don't want to talk to you,' she told him with slow emphasis.

'Chelsea, Jace told me you now know about his marriage——'

'I do now.' She pulled on her jacket with angry movements.

'Chelsea, let's talk,' he ordered firmly.

Her eyes flashed deeply blue. 'You had your chance, Lucas,' she spoke the words at him in a venomous whisper. 'You chose not to take it.'

'It wasn't my business to tell you——'

'Not even when you knew I loved you?' she accused heatedly, lowering her voice as Camilla stirred restlessly. 'You didn't tell me, Lucas, because you thought I was too juvenile to handle it. Well I'm *mature* enough to be happy that my father has found happiness, and I like Camilla very much. The only thing wrong with the whole situation is that it now means I have to be related to you!'

His mouth thinned ominously. 'You didn't think that would be such a bad idea last night.'

She blushed and then paled at the accusation. 'Last night I didn't know what a bastard you are!' she snapped back.

His mouth twisted. 'Oh, you knew, Chelsea, you've always known. But you loved me anyway——'

'Not any longer.'

'—as I love you,' he continued softly.

'Love!' She was too angry to care that he had just told her what she would have given anything to hear last night. How could he possibly love someone he wouldn't even trust with the truth! 'As you once told me, you have no conception of the word!' she told him contemptuously.

His expression became even more ominous. 'I said I love you, damn it, and I do!'

'You——'

'What on earth is going on here?' Camilla had roused completely from her sleep without either of them being aware of it, sitting up in bed to stare at them dazedly.

'Welcome to the family, Camilla.' She bent to kiss the other woman's cheek. 'I'm very pleased for you and Jace. Now if you'll excuse me,' she straightened, 'I'm going out.'

'You aren't going anywhere,' Lucas thundered.

'Lucas?' Camilla was obviously shocked by his behaviour.

'Stay out of this,' he instructed grimly. 'This is between Chelsea and me.'

'This does happen to be my bedroom,' his sister reminded him frowningly.

'In my apartment.' His eyes were glacial. 'And if I want to talk to Chelsea here then I will.'

'Well Chelsea has a say in that, buster,' Chelsea glared at him. 'And she doesn't want to talk to you here or anywhere else.'

'She's—*You're* going to,' he amended irritably. 'If I have to keep you here all day.'

'Lucas!'

'Will you stay out of this, Camilla!' he ordered impatiently.

Chelsea looked at him challengingly. 'As my step-mother I think perhaps she should hear this,' she taunted, sitting down on the bed.

'Not here, Chelsea,' he glowered at her.

'Well, I'm certainly not going to your bedroom,' she scorned.

'It's a little late to start worrying about that, isn't it,' his mouth twisted. 'And as I remember it, you didn't need forcing last time!'

She blushed at the accusation, glancing uncomfortably at Camilla. 'I could hardly have forced *you* into anything,' her voice quivered with embarrassment.

'I remember differently,' he taunted. 'Last night——'

She stood up abruptly. 'Maybe you're right,

maybe we should go and talk about this somewhere else,' she said shortly. 'I'm sure Camilla isn't interested in all this.'

'On the contrary,' the other woman settled back more comfortably on the pillows, 'I haven't been this well entertained in the morning for a long time,' she smiled at them encouragingly.

'I think I'm insulted by that remark, sweetheart,' Jace strolled into the room, smiling at his new bride as he sat down beside her on the bed, his arm about her shoulders. 'You may have returned to this bed so that you didn't embarrass Chelsea—who incidentally wasn't embarrassed at all,' he added dryly. 'But I can remember quite a few mornings when you were *very* entertained,' he reminded huskily.

'Of course, darling.' She laced her hand with his as it rested against her collar-bone. 'But you have to admit that this is something——'

'Would the two of you mind postponing this little trip down memory lane until some other time?' Lucas cut in icily.

'Of course not, you two go right ahead,' Jace invited graciously, causing Chelsea's mouth to twitch with humour, recognising the devilment in him. And Camilla seemed to be as bad, looking at them interestedly!

'We had just got to the bit where you told me you loved me,' Chelsea prompted Lucas innocently, too angry with him not to enjoy his discomfort in front of their avid audience. He looked furious!

'Now that's interesting,' Jace said as Lucas just glowered. 'Do you realise, Camilla, that if their love affair reaches its natural conclusion—which I hope its going to,' he looked questioningly at the other man. 'Then my daughter will also be our sister-in-law, and that your brother will be my son-in-law and *your* stepson-in-law, and——'

'God, this is turning into a damned farce!' Lucas scowled at them all. 'Well I hope you're all very amused.' He turned glacial eyes on Chelsea. 'I'll talk to you when you don't want an audience of clowns!'

'Oh no you don't.' She stopped him as he would have left the room. 'You've walked out on me once too often, Lucas McAdams, this time I'm walking out on you!' She strode past him, hearing Jace's chuckle of delight and Lucas's angry rebuke as she left the apartment.

CHAPTER TEN

THE past few minutes may have been amusing, but her humour faded as soon as she got outside, the smile she gave Mrs Harvey as she arrived for the day strained to say the least. She was more hurt than she cared to admit by Lucas's refusal to treat her like a responsible adult. What had he expected her to do when she learnt of his sister's marriage to her father, throw a tantrum!

And he said he loved her. God, how she wished she could believe that were true. But everything he had done last night after Jace's arrival had pointed to him merely wanting physical gratification; he had even told her that he didn't love her.

So what had happened to change his mind? Jace's arrival. Was it possible that Lucas had said he loved her because he felt guilty about their lovemaking once her father arrived? It seemed to be the only explanation. And what a heartbreaking one.

She had forgotten all about the reporters downstairs during her week of confinement to the apartment, walking into a barrage of cameras and reporters as questions were thrown at her from half a dozen different directions. She finally managed to push past them and into a cab, telling the driver to take her to the nearest park.

Early December wasn't the ideal month to be strolling through a London park at seven-thirty in the morning, the wind whipping about her bitterly chill, a frost on the ground. But at least it wasn't snowing.

She walked until she felt sure Lucas would have gone to work, squaring her shoulders as she stepped from the cab and into another barrage of questions, some of them too personal to ignore!

'Of course we're all shaken by mother's death,' she snapped at one callous young man as he questioned her emotion about the suicide.

'But your father was recently remarried, we believe,' he persisted scornfully.

'He was divorced from my mother,' she said coldly, finally pushing her way inside, never so relieved to see her father as she was at that moment, Jace stepping out of the elevator as she went to get into it.

His arms were protective about her as they went back upstairs. 'Security called and said you were being hassled,' he explained grimly.

'Some of those people,' she shuddered. 'What business is it of their's that you've remarried? You and Mom had been divorced for months——'

'They think her death was my fault, Princess,' he told her gently.

Chelsea shook her head. 'It was mine,' she choked. 'I should have been there. I——'

'Let's wait until we get inside,' Jace suggested softly. 'I think we have some things to sort out.'

The apartment was strangely silent except for the sound of Mrs Harvey working in the kitchen, Jace and Chelsea going in to the lounge, the housekeeper entering with a tray of coffee almost immediately.

Chelsea sipped the hot brew gratefully, the chill morning seeming to have entered her bones. 'Camilla and Lucas?' she questioned quietly, putting her cup down.

'Let's not worry about them for the moment,' Jace dismissed. 'I want to know what you meant just now when you said you were responsible for Gloria's death.' His eyes were narrowed questioningly.

She shuddered, her arms clasped about her knees. 'I was supposed to have gone home that— that evening before I went bowling,' she told him stiltedly. 'I only decided not to at the last moment. I did call the house, but—but there was no answer . . .' she choked back the tears as she at last admitted her guilt.

'*You* were supposed to go home that evening?' Jace repeated slowly, frowning heavily.

'Yes,' she said shakily.

'And Clare said your mother had called her to ask her to come over and collect some sewing that night too.'

'She did?' Chelsea looked puzzled.

'Mm,' Jace nodded, deep in thought. 'Clare also telephoned when her car wouldn't start and received no answer.'

'But couldn't the sewing have waited until the next day?' Chelsea frowned.

'Exactly what Clare thought,' he nodded. 'Especially when it looked as if your mother had gone out. And then we come to my own delay.'

'You were supposed to visit that evening, too?' she gasped.

'Yes,' he sighed. 'Your mother called me and told me she had to talk to me, that it was urgent. I thought she had told you about my marriage to Camilla and that you had taken it badly.'

Her eyes widened. 'Mom *knew* you were married to Camilla?'

'Yes,' he nodded. 'And I thought at the time that she had taken the news very well. It wasn't until just now that I realised she tried to manipulate me because of it.'

'What do you mean?'

'Don't you see, Chelsea, your mother had a let-out to taking those pills——'

'You realise that I know Mom committed suicide?' she gasped.

'I've had a lengthy chat with Lucas since you've been gone,' he admitted grimly. 'I was a fool to try and keep such a thing from you but——'

'You were protecting me, I know that,' she assured him gently.

'Lucas tells me that you don't need protecting, that treating you like a responsible adult would have saved a lot of heartache and confusion.'

'He should talk,' she bit out angrily.

Jace gave a half smile at her vehemence. 'We'll talk about Lucas in a moment, right now I want to clear up this situation with your mother. As I was saying, your mother had ensured that she had a let out to taking those pills,' he repeated harshly. 'She believed you were coming home, called Clare to come over, called me for the same reason, believing one of us would get there before it was too late.'

'And we all let her down,' she said dully. 'She killed herself because none of us were there to talk her out of it.'

He shook his head. 'Because none of us were there to *bring* her out of it. Don't you see, Princess, your mother didn't intend killing herself, she just wanted to punish me for marrying Camilla, probably hoped that you would blame me for her desperation, too. She didn't want to die, expected to be found by at least one of us. But you went out straight from work, Clare couldn't get to the house because her car wouldn't start, and I was delayed at the studio.'

'So we did let her down,' Chelsea insisted.

'No! Well in a way. But I should have realised when I saw how beautiful she looked, her make-up perfect, the blue nightgown——'

'It was your favourite colour on her,' Chelsea realised dazedly.

'Exactly,' he nodded. 'She did exactly the same thing last time she wanted to punish me——'

'Last time?' Chelsea gasped.

'Your mother took pills when you were twelve, too,' he told her quietly.

'I never knew. I—Was that the time you told me she had gone into hospital to have her appendix out?' Chelsea realised incredulously.

'That's it,' he confirmed.

'I wondered why Mom would never show me her scar! I thought it was because she couldn't bear the blemish on her body . . . Why did she do it?' Chelsea groaned. 'Was it something that I did?'

'No, Princess, no. Don't even think it, your mother loved you very much,' Jace soothed. 'I asked your mother for a divorce so that I could marry Camilla. Her answer was to swallow a bottle of pills,' he sighed.

'You loved Camilla even then?'

'Yes,' he admitted heavily. 'I've loved her for a very long time. But your mother wasn't strong, she——'

'She blackmailed you with the threat of suicide into staying with her!'

'She wasn't a bad woman, Princess, she just— She loved me, and she didn't want to let me go.' He shrugged. 'I agreed to stay with her if she would move back to the States with me. I thought it best to make a clean start, where I wouldn't be tempted to go to Camilla,' he admitted heavily. 'Your mother agreed, and we continued to live together.'

'You mean you sacrificed years of your life to a marriage that you knew was dead!'

He sighed. 'There was you, Princess.'

'And just how much influence did I have in your decision to stay with Mom?' Her voice was shrill at the years he had given up.

Jace grimaced. 'I couldn't bear the thought of my daughter possibly having to face the belief that I had been responsible for killing her mother.'

'But she never attempted it again, not even when you finally did divorce.'

'Because she never really believed in the divorce,' he explained gently. 'I realise that now, I realised it when I told her I had married Camilla. I fooled myself into believing she had accepted it, but she was too calm. When she killed herself I felt as guilty as hell for not realising the state of her mind. You can guess what it did to Camilla and the life we were trying to make for ourselves. I have to admit I didn't try to help her, was too caught up in my own guilt. In the end she couldn't take it any more, thought I blamed her for your mother's death.'

'That's why she came here. And that's why Lucas was so angry with her.' And why he had accused her of tying him up in the same knots her parents had the rest of his family!

'Was he?' Jace frowned. 'Well, it's all over now. I went back to the States to close up the house after Camilla left me, Clare came over to help. That was when I found out that Clare was suffering the same guilt that I was. The three of us, you, Clare, and myself, can all stay on this guilt trip if we want to, but it's going to achieve nothing. None of us, and I mean *none* of us, could have lived our lives in constant fear of your mother not liking something that we do and downing another bottle of pills!'

Chelsea was frowning. 'Why did you look at me like that when you said "none" of us?'

He sighed. 'I always suspected it was your mother's possessiveness that broke up your engagement to Randy.'

'But Mom had nothing to do with that,' she protested. 'He—— Mom said——' she broke off, pained confusion flickering across her pale face. 'Randy always said he didn't touch Mom, that she made it up,' she said dully. 'Do you think he was telling the truth?'

'I don't know,' Jace shrugged. 'I do know that your mother didn't want you to get married and leave her. I suppose I could have interfered and tried to sort out the problem, but it could have harmed your relationship with your mother. Was I wrong not to have forced the situation?'

'No,' she said heavily. 'Mom must have been a very unhappy woman.'

'When I first met her she was the most beautiful woman I'd ever seen,' Jace's expression softened. 'And she never lost that outer beauty. But inside,' he shook his head. 'It was as if her love became a sickness. She became so possessive that I had to tell her my every movement. When she became pregnant with you I feared, really feared, that she would resent you. But when you were born her possessiveness extended to you too. Maybe it was my profession that made her the way she was, or maybe she just didn't believe that I loved her, but something ate her up inside.

And it slowly, but surely killed my love for her. I still cared for her, but I could no longer love her as she needed to be loved.'

'You should never have stayed together.'

'I couldn't do that to her,' he shook his head. 'Because if I had left I would have taken you with me, and then I might as well have shoved the pills down her throat. But my love for Camilla wasn't something I welcomed; I already had enough problems in my life without falling in love with another woman. But I couldn't stop my love for her, and she felt the same way. So I decided to risk asking your mother for a divorce. I've told you what happened. Camilla was as shaken as I was by what happened, and we accepted that we had to part. But after two years we couldn't stand not being able to even see each other. By the time you reached eighteen I couldn't stand any more, and your mother was surprisingly agreeable to the idea of divorce this time; I think the fact that you chose to stay with her helped. Camilla and I were married as soon as was decently possible after the divorce.'

'Without telling me.'

'I didn't want to put you in the position of having to lie to your mother, needed a few days with Camilla before the trouble began. It wouldn't have been fair to expect you to keep it from your mother. But I knew we couldn't keep it a secret for ever, that sooner or later the media would get hold of the story, and so a few days before the—the accident I told your mother myself. She took it very calmly, even congratulated me. And she offered to tell you, said it would be better coming from her. I realise now that she was planning to take those damned pills all the time, that she perhaps hoped to turn you against

Camilla and me for hurting her so much she tried to take her own life.'

'She didn't tell me about Camilla and you,' Chelsea confirmed. 'Even though we stayed in together for a couple of evenings before she—before she died.'

'I'm sorry, Princess,' he sighed. 'Really sorry.'

'Don't be,' she hugged him. 'Mom may not have meant to kill herself this time, but sooner or later one of us would have done something to upset her and maybe that time we wouldn't have been there to stop her either.' She could see the truth of that now that she knew about the past. 'I loved Mom, still love her, but no one should live with that threat over their life, you have a right to be happy.'

'Camilla does make me very happy,' he nodded.

'Is she going to be all right?'

'I've lived through and accepted whatever responsibility I have for your mother's death, and Camilla knows that. I think she's going to be fine,' he gave a relieved smile. 'We all are. Now we just have to sort out the mess you and Lucas have made of your own relationship.'

'There is no relationship!' she told him stiffly.

His brows rose. 'And what was last night?'

'For me? The most beautiful night of my life. For Lucas? Just another sexual experience,' she dismissed disgustedly.

'He wants to marry you, Princess.'

She drew in a sharp breath. 'Did he tell you that?'

Jace shook his head. 'He asked if I minded having my brother-in-law as a son-in-law!' His mouth quirked.

'But don't you see,' she sighed. 'He's only

doing that because you know about last night and he feels guilty——'

'Like hell I am!' Lucas exploded from the direction of the kitchen.

Chelsea stepped back. 'I thought you had gone to work,' she gasped.

He scowled across the room at her. 'How could I do that with you wandering off to God knows where?' he snapped. 'I called the office and had a colleague take over my appointments for the day.'

'Jennifer Sutton?' she scorned.

His mouth twisted. 'Jennifer has decided to move on to another law firm.'

'Oh.'

'You should have seen your daughter the night she ousted Jennifer from my life, Jace,' he spoke derisively. 'She was more wickedly delightful than usual.'

'D . . . delightful?' Chelsea echoed as Jace chuckled his enjoyment.

Suddenly Lucas was smiling, more light-hearted than she had ever seen him. 'Delightful,' he nodded. 'I mean it when I told you that with you here my life is no longer dull. And I don't want you to ever leave. I want to get up with you every morning, come home to you every night——'

'Don't go any further,' Jace warned. 'Save my blushes.'

Lucas gave a disbelieving snort. 'You're even worse than your daughter when it comes to being outrageous.' His gaze returned to Chelsea. 'That evening you were waiting with my drink and asked me about my day was when I think I began to fall in love with you.'

'You mocked me,' she said with remembered pain.

'Yes,' he sighed. 'It was the only way I could stop myself from kissing you. I——'

'I'd better go,' Jace put in quietly, clasping the other man's shoulder affectionately. 'No man should have to tell a woman of his love in front of an audience.'

Lucas smiled at him. 'Believe me, it's getting easier with practice!'

'I'm sure,' Jace was chuckling as he went in search of Camilla.

There was an awkward silence once her father had left, and Chelsea looked at Lucas beneath lowered lashes, unsure what happened next, still very unsure of Lucas.

'It's been so long since someone took an interest in my life, Chelsea,' Lucas spoke softly. 'Since someone cared enough to listen, that I didn't know how to cope with it. Can you understand that?'

'I think so.' She didn't sound convinced.

'Last night,' he persisted. 'When I insisted you go back to your own room, I only did that because I wanted to face Jace with a relatively clear conscience when I told him we wanted to get married.'

'You said you didn't love me,' she reminded stubbornly.

'At that point I didn't realise I did, but when Jace arrived I wanted to protect you, tell him that we loved each other. I think I broke into a thousand pieces when you walked out on me after I told you I couldn't let you stay the night. What you had said, about waking up next to a person after making love and feeling good about it, I *knew* I felt good about it, that I wanted you there next to me for the rest of your life.'

'You didn't say any of that!'

'Because I knew you would react exactly as you did a few minutes ago; believe I made the declaration out of guilt. I felt—awkward, with Jace here, but I certainly didn't feel guilty. I love you, and I want to spend the rest of my life loving you.'

'Here?'

'Anywhere you'll be happy.'

'You thought me too immature to accept Jace's marriage to Camilla,' she accused.

'I didn't tell you out of respect for Jace's wishes. But I told him I thought he should tell you, but he insisted your mother's death had been enough of a shock for now. I had to respect his wishes, Chelsea,' he pleaded for her understanding. 'Darling, please believe me.'

'I do,' she nodded.

'But you can't forgive me,' he sighed.

'Yes, I can.'

Lucas frowned as she still regarded him steadily. 'You no longer love me?'

'Yes, I do. I always will.'

'Then what's wrong?' he groaned. 'Are you still angry with me, is that it?'

'You said I would outgrow my love for you,' she reminded.

'I'm willing to take the risk!'

'There may be no risk to take!'

'Chelsea . . .?'

Her eyes began to glow. 'Lucas, I'm still waiting for my marriage proposal,' she mocked. 'Jace assures me you want to marry me, you assure me you want to marry me, but so far no one has asked *me*!'

'Oh, darling, I forgot!' Lucas realised self-derisively. 'Will you marry me, Chelsea?' Brown eyes looked pleadingly into hers.

'Yes——'

'Darling!'

'On one condition,' she added as he took her into his arms.

'A baby by next Christmas sounds wonderful.' His strong arms strained her to him. 'I've even thought of a couple of names, how about Noelle for a girl and Christopher for a boy?'

'I like Holly for a girl better.' She was thrilled that he had actually thought about them having a baby. 'But that isn't the condition I meant.'

Lucas looked down at her frowningly. 'Then what is?'

'I want you to send the manuscript I read to a publisher—It *is* good enough, Lucas,' she insisted as he went to object. 'Anyway, what harm can it do to send it; they can only say no!'

'That's what I'm afraid of,' he grimaced.

'You aren't afraid of anything,' she scoffed. 'And then, if it's accepted, I want you to take at least a year off from your law-practice to write another one.'

'That's two conditions!'

'One long one,' she insisted, touching his cheek lovingly. 'Will you do it?'

'For you?'

'No, for you. You have to live your dreams, Lucas, because you never get a second chance. I'll never restrict you, I want you to always do what you want to do.'

'Even if I wanted to rejoin a commune?' he teased.

She laughed softly. 'You'll get enough "free love" at home!'

'I know I will. And I'll love you with everything that's in me,' he promised.

She knew that he would too, that Lucas would

make her, and any children they had, the centre of his world. He was that sort of man. 'Will you send the manuscript to a publisher? And then take a year off if it's accepted?'

'I think I'm going to need our first year together to make love to you as often as I need to.'

'Then take two years off!'

'We'll see.' His head bent and he began to kiss her, neither of them giving any more thought to the future for some time.

Their daughter Holly was born a week before Christmas the following year, the same day her father's book entered the top ten of the bestseller list. Their son Christopher was born almost a year later, when their father's second book *topped* the bestseller list!

ANNE MATHER

Anne Mather, one of Harlequin's leading romance authors, has published more than 100 million copies worldwide, including **Wild Concerto**, a *New York Times* best-seller.

Catherine Loring was an innocent in a South American country beset by civil war. Doctor Armand Alvares was arrogant yet compassionate. They could not ignore the flame of love igniting within them...whatever the cost.

HIDDEN IN THE FLAME

Enter a uniquely exciting new world with

Harlequin American Romance ^{T.M.}

Harlequin American Romances are the first romances to explore today's love relationships. These compelling novels reach into the hearts and minds of women across America... probing the most intimate moments of romance, love and desire.

You'll follow romantic heroines and irresistible men as they boldly face confusing choices. Career first, love later? Love without marriage? Long-distance relationships? All the experiences that make love real are captured in the tender, loving pages of **Harlequin American Romances.**

What makes American women so different when it comes to love? Find out with **Harlequin American Romance!**

Send for your introductory FREE book now!

Get this book FREE!

Harlequin American Romance

Twice in a Lifetime
REBECCA FLANDERS

Mail to:
Harlequin Reader Service

In the U.S.	In Canada
2504 West Southern Ave.	P.O. Box 2800, Postal Station A
Tempe, AZ 85282	5170 Yonge St., Willowdale, Ont. M2N 6J3

YES! I want to be one of the first to discover **Harlequin American Romance.** Send me FREE and without obligation *Twice in a Lifetime.* If you do not hear from me after I have examined my FREE book, please send me the 4 new **Harlequin American Romances** each month as soon as they come off the presses. I understand that I will be billed only $2.25 for each book (total $9.00). There are no shipping or handling charges. There is no minimum number of books that I have to purchase. In fact, I may cancel this arrangement at any time. *Twice in a Lifetime* is mine to keep as a FREE gift, even if I do not buy any additional books.   154 BPA BPGE

Name _____ (please print)

Address _____ Apt. no. _____

City _____ State/Prov. _____ Zip/Postal Code _____

Signature (If under 18, parent or guardian must sign.)

AMR-SUB-2R

Harlequin

INDULGE IN THE PLEASURE OF SUPERB ROMANCE READING BY CHOOSING THE MOST POPULAR LOVE STORIES IN THE WORLD

Longer, more absorbing love stories for the connoisseur of romantic fiction.

Contemporary romances— uniquely North American in flavor and appeal.

An innovative series blending contemporary romance with fast-paced adventure.

and you can never have too much romance.